DEATH TRAP

The truck driver flicked on his headlights. Lisa and Joe were caught in their glare.

"Duck," Joe said. "He's got a gun!"

His warning came too late.

There was a sharp cracking noise. Lisa gave a cry, stiffened, and fell. Joe's gut twisted. No, he thought.

The man with the gun raised his hand again.

Run—*fast,* a voice inside Joe's head cried, but he couldn't make himself move.

Another crack—and Joe felt the pain.

This time I've bought it. He swayed on his feet. Then the darkness closed in.

Books in THE HARDY BOYS CASEFILES® Series

Available from ARCHWAY Paperbacks

THE HARDY BOYS CASEFILES NO. 8

SEE NO EVIL

FRANKLIN W. DIXON

AN ARCHWAY PAPERBACK
Published by POCKET BOOKS
New York   London   Toronto   Sydney   Tokyo

AN ARCHWAY PAPERBACK *Original*

An Archway Paperback published by
POCKET BOOKS, a division of Simon & Schuster, Inc.
1230 Avenue of the Americas, New York, N.Y. 10020

ISBN: 0-671-62649-3

First Archway Paperback printing October 1987

10 9 8 7 6 5 4 3 2

THE HARDY BOYS, AN ARCHWAY PAPERBACK and
colophon are registered trademarks of Simon & Schuster, Inc.

THE HARDY BOYS CASEFILES is a trademark
of Simon & Schuster, Inc.

Printed in the U.S.A.

IL 7+

SEE NO EVIL

Chapter

1

"WHAT A JERK!" Callie Shaw muttered as she strode down the street.

She was angry at Joe Hardy, who had just said to her, "No way could we let you work with us. It wouldn't be safe for a girl—we'd wind up protecting you instead of going after the bad guys."

But Callie was even angrier with her boyfriend, Joe's brother, Frank. "I hate to admit it, Callie," he had said. "Joe's right. The characters we tangle with play rough. Bringing you on the team would be giving them a ready-made target. . . ."

All that because she had dared to suggest that Joe and Frank let her help them with their crime cases. She knew she could be an asset to them.

"I should have known better than to try to talk with you, Joe," she had said, her eyes blazing.

1

"You're the ultimate male chauvinist. The only thing you think girls are good for is to take out on dates!"

With a slight twinkle in his blue eyes, Joe said, "Well . . ."

"And *you*," Callie said, turning on Frank. "You think of me as weak and defenseless, too."

"It's not that." Frank nervously ran a hand through his dark brown hair. "It's just"—he shot a glance at Joe—"what if something happened to you? I can't ever forget what happened to Iola."

Ordinarily, that would have stopped Callie from continuing. Iola Morton had been her friend and Joe Hardy's true love. That terrible moment when Iola had died in a car blown up by terrorists changed Joe forever. Now Callie realized that it had changed Frank, too. He was really worried about her. *Too* worried about her.

Callie was fed up having to watch Frank and Joe have all the challenges, excitement, and adventures. She was fed up staying on the sidelines like a cheerleader.

Sure, she knew it could get dangerous. Callie had been horrified when Frank told her about their last case—*Deathgame*—when he and Joe had been pursued in a crazed survival game. She *knew* all that, but still she wanted to join the team. But the boys were refusing to listen to her, much less give her a try.

She had still been boiling as she started to leave Frank's house after their study date. Frank had offered to walk her home, but she told him she was perfectly capable of getting home safely—all by herself. Then she turned and stomped out the door, leaving him standing with his mouth open.

She'd let him stew awhile, she decided as she walked down the tree-lined street. The leaves had begun to change color, and the reds and yellows were intensified by the glow from the street lights. The stars were bright, and the air was crisp. Nothing disturbed the peaceful autumn night.

Then came the sound—a car driven slowly down the street behind her, its tires crunching through fallen leaves.

Callie's mouth tightened in a straight line. She knew that Joe and Frank would expect her to feel scared, walking home alone and hearing a car approach her from behind. Well, they were *wrong*. She could take care of herself. Callie forced herself to walk more slowly and to take deep breaths of the cool air.

The sound of the car drew closer.

Calm down, Callie, she told herself. It's probably just some older people driving their car extra cautiously. There was nothing odd about that, especially in a town like Bayport, where life was slow and easy. No need to walk faster. No need even to look over her shoulder. Just keep staring straight ahead. Look at the leaves in the trees. One or two were drifting down through the air. Winter was coming.

A shiver ran through her. It had to be the thought of winter. She couldn't be frightened. She was in one of Bayport's nicest, most quiet neighborhoods.

It *was* quiet, she realized. What had happened to the car? It must have turned into a driveway or down a side street. Of course, that was it.

It was so quiet that the sudden crackle of a footstep crushing leaves on the sidewalk behind her sounded as loud as a pistol shot.

Before Callie could turn around, an arm snaked across her throat in a choke hold. Then Callie saw a black leather glove appear in front of her face, holding a yellow sponge. She could smell the chloroform just before the sponge covered her nose and mouth.

For a moment Callie struggled against the vise-like grip as she desperately tried to hold her breath.

But then she had to breathe.

She struggled to keep her eyes open as the hand over her face tilted her head toward the sky.

She saw the autumn leaves above her move farther and farther away, as if she were dropping into a hole that had opened beneath her feet.

Until the last blurs of color were gone.
Until total blackness swallowed her up.

After Callie had exited, the Hardys returned to their living room and sat silently. Frank had read a book, while Joe leafed through a sports magazine.

The two of them were alone in the house while their father, the famous private detective Fenton Hardy, was in London, assisting Scotland Yard with an international art-smuggling case. Their mother and Aunt Gertrude had gone along with him, since the British had offered to pay for the family to pose as tourists as a cover for Fenton's presence.

When the phone rang abruptly, Frank leapt to answer it. "I'll get it. I bet it's Callie, calling to make up."

Joe grinned at his brother's haste.

But when Frank picked up the receiver, it wasn't Callie on the other end.

"Congratulations," said a cheerful voice. "You've been selected to receive a subscription to *Millionaire* magazine at the bargain price of seventy-five dollars a year. Yes, you, too, can get rich by following our advice. Just give me your okay, and your first issue will be in the mail next week. Plus, if you pay promptly, you'll get an autographed copy of the book *How I Made a*

Million in Pork Belly Futures by P.I. Gout. *Plus,* as a super bonus, if you pay immediately—"

Frank saw a light flashing on the phone-answering machine. Someone else was trying to get through to him. It had to be Callie.

"Look, I'm not interested in becoming a millionaire," he said into the phone. "Being dirt-poor is more my style. And I've got another call coming in. So if you'll just hang up—"

But the cheerful voice went on. "You haven't heard half of it. You'll receive your very own computer watch, so you can keep track of your profits as easily as keeping track of the time. Plus, a new updated tax guide. Plus—"

"Hey, I said goodbye," said Frank.

"A surefire way to—" the voice said, speeding up like a tape played on fast forward.

Frank slammed down the phone.

But he was too late. The incoming call light had gone off.

Maybe Callie had left a message. Frank hit the playback button on the answering machine.

There was a message—but not from Callie.

It was Callie's mother. "Hi. This is Mrs. Shaw. Please tell Callie that she left her shoulder bag with her house keys in it at home. Her dad and I are going out now, so I'll leave a key under the front doormat in case she gets back before we do. And tell her not to stay out too late. Studying for that test tomorrow won't do her much good if she's sleepy when she takes it."

The message ended there.

"Funny," said Frank, his brows furrowing. "Callie should have gotten home by now."

She probably stopped at Liz Webling's house to study," said Joe.

"I don't think so," said Frank. "She has that test tomorrow, and Liz isn't in the class."

"Maybe she went to Ernie's to do her studying over pizza and a soda," said Joe.

"Maybe," said Frank, but he still looked bothered.

"Hey, if you're worried, let's head over to Ernie's and check it out," Joe suggested. "I could go for a couple of slices with extra cheese, sausage, and pepper right now. Dueling with that girlfriend of yours works up an appetite."

"Good idea," said Frank. "Not that I'm really worried about Callie. She can take care of herself. But I would like to see her. Maybe I do owe her an apology. I mean, I was coming on a little too macho."

"Maybe." Joe looked unconvinced. "Callie kind of asked for it, though. She's trying to butt into something she doesn't know anything about. We're a team—she'd only mess us up. I'm telling you, Frank, don't let Callie change your mind about this. She could wind up walking into some

7

nasty stuff—or worse. . . ." He didn't mention Iola's name, but Frank could see the pain in his brother's eyes.

"Callie doesn't want to run my life," Frank said. "She's just looking for a challenge. And do me a favor," he went on. "Cool your opinions when we find her. You're not doing a great job of convincing her."

Frank left it at that. But he couldn't stop himself from thinking, *if* we find her.

Frank had a harder time hiding his growing concern when they arrived at Ernie's. The only person there besides the counterman was their pal Chet Morton. That was no surprise. Where there was late-night food, Chet usually was, too.

Chet looked up from the pizza platter in front of him.

"Great to see you, guys," he said to Frank and Joe. "Want to share this last slice? I can't eat the whole thing tonight."

"What's the matter? Are you on a diet?" asked Joe, grinning.

Frank wasn't in a joking mood.

"Has Callie been in here?" he asked.

"Nope," said Chet, starting on the last slice. "You supposed to meet her here?"

"Um—I was hoping to," Frank said vaguely so he wouldn't have to explain the situation. Chet was always ready to help out when the Hardys needed him, but there was no sense in getting him involved in something that might turn out to be nothing at all.

Chet nodded and took a sip of his cherry soda. As he put the glass down, he glanced up and noticed the look on Frank's face, which was mirrored on Joe's.

"What's with you two?" he asked. "You look like you've just seen a ghost."

Frank and Joe didn't answer. They were staring at the doorway, frozen. Callie—her face pale, her hair disheveled, and her eyes blinking dazedly—was swaying as she held on to the door frame for support.

Then, before Frank or Joe or Chet could move, she opened her mouth to say something.

But nothing came out.

Her grip on the door frame loosened, and she crumpled to the floor.

She lay absolutely motionless. Chet stood up, eyes wide. His hand caught the edge of the pizza platter, and the large pie plate clattered to the floor. No one noticed.

"She looks like she's—" Frank choked back the word he didn't even want to think.

Dead.

Chapter

2

JOE WAS THE first to move. Dropping to his knees at Callie's side, he grasped her wrist and felt for a pulse. It was faint, irregular, but there.

He nodded to Frank, who grabbed Chet's soda glass and dumped it out on the tabletop. He picked up a handful of crushed ice and ran to Callie, rubbing her temples with it. After a moment her eyelids fluttered open. Frank let out the breath he didn't realize he had been holding.

"Wait a second," Joe said to the counterman, who had gone to the phone. "Let's find out exactly what happened before we decide who to call."

Callie's eyes were wide open now, staring at the three faces looking anxiously into her own.

She managed a weak grin. "Hi, guys."

"Are you all right?" asked Frank.

"Yeah, what made you faint like that?" asked Joe.

"I *didn't* faint!" Callie's voice was shaky, but she was ready to resume their argument. "You probably think I saw a mouse or something."

"Forget Joe. Tell us what happened," Frank said impatiently.

Callie glanced at the counterman, who was still standing with his hand on the phone. "I'm okay," she said to him. "No need to call anybody." In a lower voice she said, "Let's sit down at a booth, where we can talk in private."

While Frank and Joe steered Callie toward a booth in the back, Chet spoke to the counterman. "Give us another big one, with the works. We've got to build up Callie's strength again."

Callie started to protest that she really wasn't hungry, but Chet cut her off quickly. "Don't worry, I'll help you eat it."

Frank waited until the four of them were settled around the table. "So what happened?" he asked Callie again.

"I'm not sure," Callie said. "I mean, I know what happened. But I have no idea *why* it happened, or who was behind it. It's a real mystery."

"Why don't you tell us about it," Joe said.

Callie took a deep breath. "While I was walking home, somebody sneaked up behind me and chloroformed me."

"Chloroformed you?" asked Frank. "You're sure?"

"I'd know the smell anywhere—I've used it in biology lab often enough, " said Callie, wrinkling her nose. "Real disgusting stuff."

"Did it knock you out?" asked Chet, his round, good-natured face shadowed with concern.

"Out like a light," said Callie. "And when I came to, everything was still pitch-black. I was seated on the ground, blindfolded, gagged, my hands tied behind me, and my feet bound."

Callie extended her hands so that the others could see her wrists. Harsh red marks still cut across them where cords had dug into her flesh recently.

"Ouch," said Frank. "How did you get free?"

"I was still woozy." Callie's face tightened as the scene came back to her. "It was like a dream—a nightmare. I could tell I was in some kind of open space. Then I felt something hard jutting up against my back. A rock. I wiggled the cords against it until I cut through them and got my hands loose. The rest was easy."

"Where were you?" asked Frank, touching Callie's wrist tenderly. Besides the welts from the cords, he could see abrasions where the rock had rubbed against her skin.

"In a vacant lot a couple of blocks from here," Callie said. "I could see the light from this place when I finally made it to the sidewalk. Good thing Ernie's stays open late. I was still kind of out of it, and I just made it here when—well, you saw what happened."

Joe cleared his throat. "Uh, Callie, I didn't mean anything when I said—er—you know, about you fainting and all—"

"Sure, Joe," said Callie dryly. "You didn't say anything that I didn't expect from you."

"I'm glad to see you're back to normal, anyway," Joe said back, with a grin.

Frank interrupted them. "We know who to call now—the police. This is one time having Collig's private number will come in handy."

Ezra Collig was the Bayport police chief. The Hardys had helped him with some cases in the past, and he had given them his private phone number in case he was needed in a hurry.

"It's too late to get Collig now," Joe said. "We'll have to wait until tomorrow morning."

"Maybe Riley's on duty," said Frank. He was talking about Con Riley, one of Bayport's finest and the Hardys' best contact on the force.

Joe shook his head. "Huh-uh. Riley's on vacation."

"But we can't wait," Callie said, protesting. "We have to get on the trail while it's still hot."

Frank and Joe exchanged glances, then grins.

"Joe and I aren't thinking about waiting until tomorrow to do something," Frank said.

13

"Yeah," said Joe, his eyes gleaming with anti-cipation.

"So, if you could tell us where that empty lot is—" The same gleam lit Frank's eyes.

"Hey, wait a second, guys," Callie said. "I won't *tell* you where it is. But I'll *show* you. No way you're leaving me out of *this* investigation. Come on, let's go."

Just then the pizza arrived.

"Great," said Chet. "We'll polish this off and be on our way."

"No time for that," said Frank, getting up.

"Maybe we can have it packed up to go," Chet suggested, desperation in his voice.

"No time for that, either," said Joe. "We'll have to settle for a slice each, to eat as we walk." He grabbed a slice and stood up.

"None for me," said Callie, getting to her feet. "Chloroform is a great appetite killer."

"But that leaves five big slices—well, four, if I grabbed two," said Chet.

Finally Frank took pity on him. "Maybe you should stay here and finish it. If we all go, the counterman will get suspicious. We should keep this operation undercover for the time being."

Chet looked relieved. "Okay. Don't worry, I'll do my part. I'll finish this pizza as if I didn't have anything else on my mind."

"I knew I could count on you," Frank said,

grabbing a slice for himself before he, Joe, and Callie headed out of Ernie's. As they passed the counterman, Frank thanked him for his help. "Callie's just got some kind of virus. We'll make sure she gets home okay."

The counterman grunted, then yawned. He looked at his watch, then at Chet attacking the pizza. At the rate Chet was devouring those slices, he'd be out of there on time.

The Hardys and Callie soon reached the vacant lot. Frank pulled a pen-size flashlight from his pocket and flicked it on. "Let's take a look."

Callie bent over, following the beam of light as it moved across the ground. "Yes, there's my calculus book," she called. "And my history book. And there's my notebook."

The books lay near one another on the ground. Callie picked them up and examined them.

"Hey, watch out. You're forgetting about fingerprints." Joe reached for the books.

"The guy was wearing gloves," said Callie, not bothering to look away from the book she was examining. "My books are all okay. But the way they're lying open makes me think the guy riffled through them. I wonder what he was looking for."

"Money, probably. Good thing you didn't have your shoulder bag with you."

"I have to hand it to you, you've got sharp

eyes," Callie said. "I didn't realize I had forgotten it till I was almost at your place tonight. By then I didn't feel like going home to get it."

"Joe's sharp eyes have nothing to do with it," Frank said, earning a dirty look from his brother. "After you left, your mom called to say you had left the bag at home and she was leaving the front door key under the doormat."

"Right. They were going to a surprise birthday party for an old friend," said Callie. "They won't be home until late." She turned to Joe. "I take back the compliment. Sharp eyes—hah!"

"They're sharp enough to see what happened here," said Joe. "The mugger desperately went through your books, hunting for cash. He must have been pretty mad, getting nothing for his trouble."

"He sure did go to a lot of trouble." Frank frowned. "Using chloroform for a simple mugging."

"It *is* unusual," Joe admitted. "But what could he have wanted besides her bag? There's no reason for anyone to attack Callie—she's no one special."

Callie glared at him. "Thanks a lot, Joe," she muttered.

"Oh, you know what I mean," Joe replied.

"At least you didn't get hurt, Callie." Frank took her hand. "We can be thankful for that."

"I'd be more thankful for some clues," Callie

said. "This guy left no fingerprints, and I didn't see his face. Quite a challenge, huh?"

"Maybe an impossible one for the time being." Frank made one last sweep with his flashlight before giving up. "I don't think there's anything we can do until the mugger strikes again. Dad says that most crooks are basically unimaginative. They choose one method of operation and keep using it over and over. So maybe we'll be able to spot the pattern when this guy tries his next heist."

"We'll just keep on the lookout," said Joe, agreeing.

Callie yawned. "Well, if there's nothing more to do right now, I'm heading home to bed," she said. "Mugging or no mugging, I still have that exam tomorrow. And the one thing I can't afford to have stolen is sleep."

"We'll walk you home," said Frank, taking her arm. "You must still feel pretty shaken up."

But the way he took her arm, holding it as if she were made of fragile china, made Callie shake him off.

"Thanks, but, no thanks," she said. "I can make it by myself. You think lightning will strike twice in one night?" She turned away, about to head off. Then she turned back to Frank. "If you want any help hunting this guy, give me a call. Otherwise, I'll be pretty busy this week."

Frank watched her walk away from them with a determined stride.

"Still a little angry, I guess," Joe said. "Don't worry. It'll blow over."

"You don't know Callie," said Frank. "That was her I-hate-to-lose look. She gets it whenever I pull ahead of her in a game." Frank grinned. "The only person I know who's more competitive is you."

"Well, *somebody* beat her out," said Joe. "That mugger. But I doubt she'll learn from it."

Frank stopped walking. "Look, Joe, lay off!" He turned to face his brother. "I don't know what your problem is, but you've really been on Callie's case lately. She's into something dangerous—and it's up to *us* to help her out. If you keep going on at her, she'll go off on her own and take stupid risks, just to prove that she's not helpless. Why can't you just leave her alone?"

"*Me* leave *her* alone? Every time I turn around she's telling me I'm just a dumb jock with a football for a brain. Frank, we're supposed to be a team, remember? But Callie is turning us into a *debating* team!" Joe paused, trying to cool down a little. "Don't you care—"

Frank cut him off. "What I care about right now is Callie," he said. "And I'm going to make sure nothing else happens to her." Angrily, he turned and began to walk again, his strides long.

Joe stared after Frank for a minute. Then, muttering under his breath, he ran to catch up.

Callie was still seething as she walked home. Somehow, she had to cure Frank of his stupid idea that she was fragile and defenseless.

Then a thought struck her. If she could find the mugger *before* Frank and Joe did . . . if she could track him down and identify him to the police . . .

That might be the exact lesson Frank needed. It would be nice if it taught Joe something, too, but she didn't expect that much. Joe was impossible.

She'd start the next day. Her friend Liz Webling could help. Liz's dad was editor of the Bayport *Times,* and Liz had instant access to all the past editions and their crime reports. Besides, Liz wanted to be an investigative reporter and had great instincts at sniffing out news. Yes, she decided, Liz would be a definite asset.

But first things first, Callie reminded herself. She had to get a good night's sleep, then she had to take her calculus test. After that she could test her instincts and abilities as a detective.

When Callie arrived home the house was dark. Her parents still hadn't returned. She lifted the doormat and felt for the key.

It wasn't there.

Funny, she thought. Her mom forgot about it.

She was probably running late for the party. Maybe she left the door open, though. Callie turned the knob.

The door swung open.

"Thank goodness," Callie said out loud. Now she could go straight up to her room and get to bed.

But Callie didn't make it any farther than the threshold.

A man stood in front of her.

His black stocking mask kept her from seeing his face, and a heavy black sweater and baggy jeans masked his weight. But she recognized the black gloves on his hands. The black gloves that had clamped down over her mouth earlier that evening. The black gloves that were reaching for her again now.

She had found her mugger.

Or rather, he had found her.

And this time, she knew, he didn't plan on letting her go alive.

Chapter

3

CALLIE HAD ONLY one weapon to defend herself with—her voice. And she used it. Her scream was earsplitting.

The mugger froze for just a second, then decided. He brushed past Callie, knocking her off balance, spinning her halfway around. By the time she recovered and tried to get another look at him, he had disappeared into the night.

She felt as if she would explode, so she stood motionless until she had calmed down enough to think clearly again.

Then she went inside, closed and locked the door, and moved to the phone.

She punched out a number and was relieved when Frank answered it on the first ring.

"Can you come over here now?" she asked.

"Callie, are you all right?" asked Frank. "What's up?"

"The mugger," said Callie. "He was wearing a mask, but I'm sure it was him. He was here when I got home. I screamed and scared him off. He must have been afraid of the neighbors arriving. Good thing he didn't know that the Joneses are away and Mrs. Cole is deaf."

"But why, I wonder?" Frank said.

"That's what I thought you might help me figure out," said Callie.

"I'll be right over," said Frank.

Ten minutes later Frank knocked gently on the door, Joe beside him.

"Relax, Callie," Joe said. "The Hardys are here. Your troubles are over."

"Cut it out, Joe. I figured two heads would be better than one," Frank said to Callie.

"You mean, three heads would be better than two," said Callie in an icy tone. "Or don't you count me as one?"

"Listen, there's no way I'm going to get cut out of a mystery," Joe said.

"Why not? You're always trying to cut *me* out." Callie shook her head. "Maybe you guys shouldn't have come over. I'd probably be better off by myself."

"Hey, I'm sorry. What I said didn't come out the way I meant it," Frank said. "But we're not going to get anything done if you keep flying off the handle." He looked at Joe. "Either of you."

Callie nodded. "Let's see if we can figure out what's going on."

"Start with what happened here," said Frank. "Where was the guy?"

"He was inside the house."

"So he was waiting for you when you arrived." Frank frowned.

"No, I don't think he was *waiting* for me," said Callie. "Otherwise he wouldn't have left the door unlocked behind him. He had to believe I was still tied up in that vacant lot. He must have made a lucky guess and found the key under the mat."

"I see you have this worked out already," said Frank with affectionate admiration.

"Yeah, your theory sounds good as far as it goes," Joe had to admit. "But now comes the hard part. Why would this guy first mug you, then come to burgle your house? There has to be a link."

"He probably got my address from my books," Callie said. "But I really am stumped. What does he want from me? Why'd he go to all the trouble of coming here after grabbing me on the street?"

"Did he do much damage?" asked Frank, glancing around the comfortable living room. "Nothing looks disturbed."

"That's another weird thing," said Callie. "He

seems to have been careful not to leave any trace that he was here. Except for the downstairs hall closet, which was a real mess. Maybe he was in the middle of searching it when he heard me at the front door."

"Maybe he had only just arrived himself, and that was the first place he hit," said Joe. In spite of himself, he was interested.

"I thought that myself—until I spotted this," said Callie. She went to the magazine rack and pulled out a bunch of magazines. "My dad is a nut about keeping magazines in the rack in chronological order—he says it saves him time when he's looking for an article he wants to read. My mom and I go along with him. She says everyone is entitled to at least one mania. But the magazines are out of order now. Which means the mugger must have gone through them, then replaced them. Obviously he thought no one would know he had touched them."

"He didn't figure on you," said Frank.

"Yeah, you're good at spotting little details like that," said Joe. "But we have to worry about the big picture. What was the guy doing here? What was he looking for? That'll take brain power. Deduction. Fortunately, that's Frank's specialty."

"First, let's consider Callie's mugging," Frank said. "The mugger was after something—but did he get it?"

Callie shook her head. "My shoulder bag was here at home. All I was carrying were my schoolbooks. And we found those."

"So it had to be something that the mugger didn't find," said Frank. "What was it?"

Callie had an answer before Frank could say it. "It had to be something in my bag, which I almost always carry."

"Right," said Frank, nodding. "Let's say it was your purse. When the mugger discovered you didn't have it, he tied you up so he'd be free to break into your house. The obvious next question is, what could you have in your shoulder bag that's worth all that?"

Callie shook her head. "I have no idea." Then, abruptly, her eyes brightened. "Maybe that's the point! Maybe I've got something in my bag that I *wouldn't* miss if it were stolen. That could be why the mugger was trying to hide the fact that he'd been here. That way, he could lift whatever it was he was after and get away with it with nobody being the wiser."

"I couldn't have put it better myself," said Frank. "Or figured it out faster."

"So let's take a look at that famous shoulder bag and check out what's in it," Joe said.

"Where is your bag?" Frank asked Callie. "If it's still here, that is."

"I'm pretty sure he didn't get it," said Callie. "He didn't get that far. He was still downstairs when I interrupted him, and my bag is in my room upstairs. That's where my mom always puts anything that I leave lying around."

"Let's go," said Joe, turning toward the stairs.

"Uh, maybe I'd better bring it down here," said Callie, looking embarrassed. "My room is kind of a mess."

"That won't bother us," said Joe.

"We should check out your room, anyway," said Frank. "There's a chance that the mugger was there. He might have left some clues."

Callie shrugged. "Okay. But don't say I didn't warn you."

Frank saw what she meant as soon as they entered her room.

"Wow, you make Joe look neat," said Frank, surveying the jumble of books, papers, records, clothes, high heels, jogging shoes, a gleaming set of barbells, and a cluster of scruffy stuffed animals.

"And I thought girls were supposed to be neat," said Joe, shaking his head in wonderment.

"Another myth shattered," said Callie. She found her bag where her mother had put it, on the last remaining clear spot on her overloaded desk.

"See any signs of disturbance in the room?" Frank asked as he stared around the room. "I guess that would be hard to answer."

"Not hard at all," said Callie. "It might look like chaos to you, but it's home to me. I know

26

every square inch of this mess." She gave the room a quick once-over with her eyes, then said, "Nothing I can see out of place. Of course, I'll have to check through my bag to make sure nothing is missing."

"I'm looking forward to that," said Joe. "I've always wondered what girls carry in these things."

"Curiosity killed the cat," said Callie. "Okay, let's take it downstairs. It'll be easier to sort out the stuff there. We're going to need room."

Callie started piling the contents of her bag on the living room coffee table, checking out the items one by one.

"Let's see," she said. "Calculator. New address book. Old address book. Still older address book. Tissues. Eyeliner. Paperback thriller. Pen. Pen. Pencil. Pencil. Sunglasses. Folding umbrella." Then she stopped, with the bag still half-full. "Hey, what's this?" She pulled out a small black book.

"Not yours?" asked Frank.

"Never saw it before," said Callie.

"Let's see what's in it," said Joe.

Callie opened it and began turning the pages. "It's a calendar notebook," she said. "Some of the pages are blank. Others have entries—a lot of letters and numbers that don't make sense."

Frank was looking over her shoulder. "It's probably some kind of code."

27

"How did this get in your bag?" Joe asked.

"No idea," Callie said, without looking up from the book. "If we could decipher some of these entries, then maybe we could figure out how the book got in my bag."

"We could run them through my computer," said Frank. "All I have to do is work out a decoding program. That shouldn't be too hard."

"We don't have to go to that trouble," said Callie. "This code doesn't look all that complicated." She picked up her school notebook and started copying entries into it. "Each entry is a short series of letters followed by a longer series of numbers. And some of the entries on different pages are exactly alike."

"Why waste brain power when we have computer power?" Frank gestured impatiently. He felt about his computer the way some people feel about their pets. He not only liked to play with it, he felt it was his duty to keep it well exercised and fed.

"I like to depend on my own energy supply instead of something that comes out of a socket," said Callie. She was already studying the letters and numbers she had scribbled down. The tip of her tongue flicked across her upper lip, as it always did when she was concentrating extra hard.

It was a look that Frank knew from when Callie went all out to try to beat him in one of their

fiercely contested chess matches. He also knew
that there was no talking to her right then. When
Callie decided to work out a problem, nothing
short of an earthquake could divert her.

He was wrong this time, though.

It didn't take an earthquake.

Just the lights suddenly going out, plunging the
room into total darkness.

A sound told them that someone was in the
room with them.

Chapter

4

SEVERAL THINGS SEEMED to happen all at once. But they really happened one right after another, like a string of firecrackers going off one by one.

The glare of a high-intensity light shattered the darkness, blinding Joe and Frank and Callie.

Dazed and blinking, Joe threw himself at the light, to tackle whoever was holding it.

A kick slashed across his ankles, knocking his feet out from under him. And at the same instant a swift, axlike chop against the back of his neck sent him sprawling forward. His head smacked against the wall.

Joe was already in never-never land as Frank was leaping to his aid. He ran into the steel-tipped toe of a boot, which scored a direct hit on his chin.

When Joe came to, he felt something cold and wet against his forehead. Cautiously he opened his eyes. The normal lights in the room were back on, and he was lying on the floor. Callie was on her knees next to him, pressing a cold compress against his forehead, a concerned look in her eyes.

When she saw his eyes flicker open, she said, "Don't move. You might have a concussion."

Joe touched his forehead and shook his head gingerly.

"What?" he asked. "A little bump like this? No way would this stop me." He raised himself on his elbow, then fell back as the room began to spin.

Callie sighed and stood up. "I should have guessed your skull would be too thick to be seriously damaged." She turned to Frank, who was standing and rubbing his jaw. "How do you feel?"

"Still shaky—but nothing seems to be broken," Frank said. "You okay?"

"While you two were diving at the intruder, I dove for the floor," Callie said. "He didn't seem interested in me. He got what he was after—the black book we found."

"Did you get a look at him?" Frank asked.

Callie shook her head. "No. He shut off the light he was carrying as soon as he knocked you two out. And before my eyes could adjust to the darkness, he must have spotted the black book on the table. That was all he had to see. He grabbed it and was gone. The guy moved like lightning."

"And he had a kick like a mule," said Frank, touching his jaw.

"He sure knew his stuff—not many goons could throw me like that," said Joe. Slowly he pulled himself up. "What beats me is how he got in here so quietly."

"He was nice enough to provide the answer to that. He left this on the coffee table where the black book used to be," said Callie. She held up the front-door key. "He must have taken it with him when I surprised him earlier."

"That makes sense," said Frank. "But why would he bother returning it?"

"Maybe it's his way of telling us that he won't be a threat anymore—now that he has what he wants," Callie said speculatively. "Maybe he was saying that we should forget what happened, and we'd never be bothered by him again." She paused. "Or maybe he just wants us to think that, so we'll lower our guards."

"He doesn't know who he's dealing with." Joe's voice was grim. His hands were clenched in fists.

"The trouble is, he does," said Frank. "He knows where Callie lives. And now that he's gotten a look at us, it won't be hard for him to find out who we are, too. It isn't easy to lose yourself in Bayport."

"That works two ways," said Joe. "If this guy can find out who we are, we can find him, too."

"Except that right now he has the upper hand—he knows a lot more about us than we do about him," said Frank. "Which reminds me—" He went to the windows and drew the blinds. "He might still be out there, for all we know."

"I don't see why," said Joe. "He got what he was after. What else could he want?"

"He might want *this*," said Callie as she produced a crumpled sheet of paper. On it were the entries she had copied from the black book. "I ripped the page out of my notebook before I dove for the floor. He must have been watching us through the window and seen me copying, because he grabbed my notebook along with the black book. I wonder what he's going to do with my American history notes. Maybe I can get him to write my report for me."

"Good work," said Frank. "Now we can decode those entries and start to find out who and what we're dealing with."

"But first I have to figure out—" Callie began to say, when the sound of the front door opening stopped her.

All of them tensed, until they heard Callie's dad call out, "Hi, we're home. Hey, are you kids hitting the books over here now?'' he said, walking into the room. "I have to admit, when I was your age, I was never that studious."

"Oh, we finished studying awhile ago," Callie said. "Frank and Joe walked me home."

"That was very nice of you boys," Mrs. Shaw said. "I know Callie thinks I worry too much, but I don't like her walking home alone at night."

"In Bayport?" Mr. Shaw said, smiling. "Come on, dear, I don't think there's much cause for concern."

"How was the party?" Callie asked quickly.

"Actually, not much fun," her dad replied.

"Why?" Callie asked. "Wasn't Mr. Carey surprised by the party? Or didn't he like to be reminded of his birthday?"

"It wasn't that," said her dad. "You know he's a civil-court judge, and like everybody else in the city government, he was pretty upset by what happened today. In fact, that was all anyone at the party was talking about."

"Happened today?" asked Frank. "What happened?"

"Didn't you hear?" asked Callie's mom. "The story was on all the local news broadcasts this evening."

"We were too busy studying," Callie said quickly. "Tell us what happened."

"Pretty grim news, I'm afraid," her dad said.

34

"Jack Morrison was found dead in his office at City Hall."

"That's terrible," said Callie.

"Yes, it is," Mrs. Shaw said. "But the real tragedy is that Mr. Morrison committed suicide."

For a moment no one said anything. Jack Morrison had been the Bayport city manager for the past four years. Friendly, popular, with a talent for getting his picture on the front page, he was considered a shoo-in for reelection to a new term.

"I was in City Hall just this afternoon," said Callie. "I picked up an application for a full driver's license for when I turn eighteen. I'm surprised I didn't see any commotion."

"His body wasn't discovered until about five-thirty," Mr. Shaw explained. "Morrison was locked up in his office. His secretary went in to say good night and found him. The coroner said he'd been dead three or four hours by then."

"Are they sure it was suicide?" asked Frank.

"No doubt of it." Mr. Shaw shook his head sadly. "There was a gun with a silencer in his hand. And powder burns next to the wound on his temple. It must have been gruesome."

"But *why?*" Callie asked. "Was there a note?"

Her dad shook his head. "Apparently not."

"That's unusual," Frank mused out loud. "Suicide victims almost always leave notes."

"I'd just as soon drop the subject," Mrs. Shaw said. "It's all I've been hearing about for the past few hours, and it's just too depressing. Besides, I'm sure we can trust the police to tie up the loose ends."

"I guess you're right. There's nothing we can do," Frank said slowly. He wasn't going to pursue it—this was not the time. But he did wonder why the police hadn't found a note.

"One thing you kids can do is get some sleep," said Mrs. Shaw.

"Right," said Joe, taking the hint. "I've got football practice tomorrow afternoon."

"Good night, Mr. Shaw, Mrs. Shaw," Frank said. "See you tomorrow, Callie."

It was only after Joe and Frank left the house and were walking home that Frank remembered. "Hey, Callie didn't give me that paper with the coded entries she copied down."

"She probably forgot in the excitement of that news about Morrison," said Joe.

"Maybe," said Frank. "And maybe not. You know Callie. I bet she kept that paper on purpose. Just so she can take a crack at the code on her own." He shook his head. "Once you start Callie's competitive juices flowing, it's real hard to shut them off."

"You know her better than I do," said Joe, shrugging.

Frank squinted at Joe. "You know what?" he

36

said. "You two are exactly alike. That's why you always try to top each other."

"We are *not* alike. And I'm not trying to top anyone, even if Callie is. She's got a chip on her shoulder because she's a girl. For some reason, she's taking it out on me," Joe replied.

"You're as stubborn as a mule," Frank said.

"You mean, I'm as stubborn as Callie," Joe retorted.

They walked in silence for a while. Then Frank brought up the topic that had been bothering him since they'd heard about Jack Morrison's death.

"What about Morrison's not leaving a note?" he asked.

Joe opened his mouth, but he never got a chance to reply.

A female scream sliced through the night.

Both Hardys thought the same thing instantly, but Frank said it first: "Callie!"

"She followed us to give us that paper!" Joe said.

"She's been jumped!" said Frank.

"The mugger!" said Joe.

The Hardys dashed back the way they had come. Another scream sounded, even louder than the first one. Then silence followed.

Frank's voice was hoarse. "We're already too late!"

Chapter

5

"SHE MANAGED TO get away!" Frank gasped in relief as he and Joe rounded a corner and saw a girl running toward them.

Then the girl passed under a streetlight, and even a block away, they could see that it wasn't Callie.

Her platinum blond hair was cut short and spiky. She wore a tan trenchcoat, and her lipstick was a bright scarlet slash in sharp contrast to her pale skin.

As Frank and Joe got closer to the girl, they could see that she was beautiful—and terrified.

Finally they met in the middle of the block. The girl threw her arms around Joe and clung to him, gasping for breath, limp with relief.

"Good thing you guys showed up when you

did," she said while taking large gulps of air. "I thought for sure he'd get me."

"Who was after you?" asked Frank.

His question seemed to snap her out of her panicked state. She let her arms drop away from Joe and stepped back from him.

"Oh, I'm sorry," she said to Joe. "I was just so scared. I grabbed you like you were a life preserver or something."

"That's okay," he said, assuring her. He looked more closely at her then. And he liked what he saw. She had to be one of the most beautiful girls he had ever been near.

Actually, though, he thought, she wasn't exactly a girl. She looked older—in her early twenties. Not that that was old, of course.

He smiled into her eyes, but Frank's business-like voice cut through the moment. "This guy who tried to mug you—what did he look like? Which way did he go?"

"I couldn't see his face—he wore a stocking mask. He jumped at me from the shadows and grabbed at my bag. I screamed and started running. He came running after me. Then I turned the corner and saw you guys. He must have seen you, too, and taken off. Anyway"—she gave a nervous glance down the deserted street—"he's gone now."

"Good thing you could run fast," Frank said.

"Yes, I was on the track team in college. Ran

the hundred-yard dash," she said. "But I wasn't about to try to match muscles with this guy. It's nice to know there are guys like *you* around to protect me."

"Anytime," Joe assured her. "By the way, what's your name?"

"Lisa," she said. "Lisa Cantwell."

"Do you live around here?" Joe asked.

"No, I'm from New York City," she said.

"You're visiting someone then?" Joe asked. Then he added as casually as he could, "A boyfriend?"

"No, I don't know a soul in town," Lisa said. Joe did his best to mask his relief. "I'm here on a job. At least, what I hope is a job. I'm a freelance journalist, or trying to be one, anyway. I have to admit, I haven't had much luck since I got out of college last spring."

Last spring, thought Joe. That would make her twenty-one. Twenty-two at the oldest. That wasn't so old. But, he reminded himself, he wasn't interested in girls. Not since Iola. But if he were interested, he could like this beautiful girl.

"Are you applying for a job on the paper here?" Frank asked.

"Not on your life." She smiled apologetically. "Bayport's a nice little place. But I'm a city girl. What brought me here is a bit of news I heard a few hours ago. The suicide of your city manager.

Sounded like it could turn into a nice story, a story I could sell. So I hopped on the first train here, figuring I'd sniff around."

"Well, you sure ran into action right away." Joe grinned.

"But not the kind I'm looking for," said Lisa. "A run-of-the-mill mugging doesn't make the front page in the Big Apple. What I'm after is something big. When a pol does a number on himself, you can sometimes find a big story behind it. We're talking headlines like 'Scandal Explodes in All-American Town.' I was walking around here tonight, trying to get some background material. A feel for the setting. You know, a peaceful, respectable, law-abiding town with turmoil underneath."

Lisa paused for a second. "Fine investigative reporter I am. I've been talking on and on, and I haven't even found out your names."

"I'm Joe Hardy. This is my brother Frank."

"Hardy? Hardy?" Lisa said with a puzzled look. "I've heard that name."

"Maybe you've heard about our father, Fenton Hardy," said Frank.

"Of course, that's it," said Lisa, her face brightening. "The famous detective. He's practically a legend. And you two are his sons?"

"That's us, chips off the old block, as he likes to say," said Joe. Normally he and Frank kept

41

quiet about their own investigating activities. But in this case he wanted Lisa to know that he wasn't just an ordinary teenager.

Lisa looked at him with new interest. "I bet you've learned a lot, being around your dad."

Ignoring the stern look that Frank shot him, Joe answered her. "You're right about that. In fact, we've done more than learn. We've done a few things on our own. Quite a few things."

"I can see that," said Lisa warmly. "You knew what you were doing when you came to my rescue. I can use help tracking down this story. Help from somebody who knows this town—and who knows basic detective work. Somebody who can protect me if it gets dangerous. Somebody like you two guys. I'd be really grateful. More than grateful—I'd give you a cut of whatever I made on the story, assuming I can sell it."

Before Joe could answer, Frank spoke up, "Sorry, but we're pretty busy right now. I'm not free to tell you what the case is, but—"

Joe cut him off quickly. "Speak for yourself, Frank." Then he turned to Lisa. "My brother has problems with his priorities, but I don't. If you want me to help, you don't have to scream. Just whistle, as they say."

"Suppose I just phone?" Lisa said, smiling. Her lively blue eyes looked slightly mischievous.

"That, too," said Joe, smiling back at her.

"Great," said Lisa. She pulled a notepad and pen from her bag. "What's your phone number and address?"

Joe gave them to her, ignoring the warning glances Frank was shooting at him.

Lisa ignored Frank, too. She had eyes only for Joe as she copied down his number and address. Putting the notepad in her bag, she said, "I'll be in touch. You know the movie *Casablanca*? 'This could be the beginning of a beautiful friendship.' "

They said goodbye, and Joe watched her walk away.

"Definitely beautiful," he said, shaking his head.

Frank interrupted his pleasant thoughts. "Hey, what's the big idea? We've got Callie to worry about. That's a full-time job."

"Maybe for you, but not me," Joe said. "It looks like that mugger wasn't just interested in Callie. He went after Lisa, too. And we don't know how many others he's attacked or will try to attack. Besides, Callie's made it clear that she can take care of herself. If you want to go on helping somebody who isn't even going to thank you, that's your business. As for me, I'd rather go where I'm wanted. By a girl who appreciates what I'm doing for her."

"If anything happens to Callie—" Frank said.

"Don't worry, I'll pitch in to protect her if I'm needed," Joe said, interrupting him. "But I'm helping Lisa out, too."

"Joe, something doesn't add up here," Frank said slowly. "There's something very weird about this case. We decided he was after the black book that was stashed in Callie's bag. Right?" Joe nodded. "He's not a common mugger. Then why would he try to snatch Lisa's bag, too? I have a feeling we're getting into something *big*."

"Maybe so," Joe replied. "All the more reason for me to stick with Lisa. If we are on to something major, she's definitely going to need help. She's got to be involved, too."

"Yes, but how? She just popped up out of nowhere," Frank said.

"The only way to find out is to hang around her," Joe said, grinning.

Frank and Joe were silent for the rest of the way home. Each was lost in his own thoughts.

Frank was thinking of Callie. He'd bet anything she hadn't gone to sleep yet, despite her mom's urgings. He grinned at the thought of Callie pretending to go to bed, then attacking the code as soon as her bedroom door was closed.

Either that, or she'd try to figure out how the black book had gotten in her shoulder bag in the first place. She'd go over every move she made, thinking back in time until she remembered what she needed to know. She wouldn't rest until she had solved both problems, or until she had to go downstairs for breakfast. He just hoped that she'd call him, though, as soon as she figured out anything.

As they walked, Joe was thinking about Lisa. She was totally different from Iola, but the feeling she sparked in him was the same. He knew why he had liked her immediately—Lisa obviously liked adventure. She wasn't afraid of danger if that's where the action led her.

And she clearly needed Joe around to help her out of trouble. A difference of a few years in age wasn't going to stop him from getting to know her better. And judging by the way she had looked at him, Joe didn't think it would stop Lisa, either. What a dynamite team they'd make.

He hoped that she would call him quickly, to let him in on her investigation of the scandal brewing in Bayport. No doubt she'd be tangling with trouble again, and he was eager to help her out.

"Home, sweet home," Frank said as he opened the front door of the Hardys' house.

"It sure feels funny with everybody away," said Joe as he followed his brother inside.

Then the phone rang.

"I'll get it!" Frank exclaimed.

"No, I'll get it!" said Joe.

They raced for it.

Chapter

6

FRANK WON—IN two ways.

He was a step closer to the phone when it rang, so he beat Joe to it. And when he picked it up, Callie was on the other end.

"I've got it!" she announced.

"You've broken the code?" he asked.

"Not yet, though I'm working on it," she said. "But I did figure out where I could have gotten that black book."

"Great! Where?" asked Frank.

"I went over in my mind everything I did yesterday, everywhere I went, and finally—"

Then Callie's mom broke into the connection. "Callie, is that you on the phone? Tomorrow is a schoolday. Don't forget your calculus test."

Frank could hear Callie's loud sigh. "Look,

there's no sense trying to fill you in before my mom cuts in again. We'll meet at Ernie's after school tomorrow. I'll give you the whole story."

"Fine," said Frank. "And bring along that sheet of paper. I can take it home and run it through my computer."

"Okay—if I haven't broken the code by then."

After Callie hung up, Frank told Joe about the conversation. "Don't be surprised if you see Callie rubbing her eyes tomorrow. I'll bet she stays up all night with that piece of paper. Well, let's hit the sack. We have a big day tomorrow, too."

The phone rang again, just after the boys made it upstairs.

"My turn." Joe grabbed the extension.

"Hey, Callie," he said, not waiting for the person on the other end to speak. "We're growing boys. We need our sleep. Why don't you try getting some, too? Wait until tomorrow to tell us what you've found out, and we'll get on the case right away. No sweat."

"Callie? Who's Callie?" asked the voice on the other end.

"Lisa?" said Joe.

"Right," Lisa said. "But if you're expecting a call, I'll phone back—"

"No, not at all," Joe said hurriedly, before she could hang up. "Callie is Frank's girlfriend. She was attacked tonight, too. Probably by the same

47

guy who jumped you. Callie's got kind of a vivid imagination, though. I thought you were her calling with another crazy idea about why she was attacked. There was this little black book the mugger took—"

"Black book?" Lisa asked. "That sounds interesting! What sort of black book?"

"It *is* pretty interesting," said Joe, agreeing. He suddenly felt friendlier toward Callie. Leaning back in his chair, he stretched out his legs. "The book was full of coded entries. Somehow, it wound up in Callie's bag." He told Lisa about the three attempts the mugger had made on Callie. "She only managed to copy out one page of the code," he finished up. "We're going to see if we can decipher it when we get together tomorrow afternoon. If Callie could figure out where she got the book, we'd really have something to go on."

"You think this might be part of something bigger?" Lisa asked.

"Exactly," said Joe, admiring her quick understanding. "Now, if Callie just won't call again tonight, we can all get some sleep and start on the case tomorrow all rested up."

"Maybe I shouldn't have called," said Lisa. "I mean, I don't want to be a bother. I decided I could really use your help on this story. I'm a total stranger in this town, and I don't have much time to get my bearings. I thought we might set up a meeting, and you could fill me in on Bayport. But if it's too much trouble—"

"Not on your life," said Joe, ignoring his brother, who had been following the conversation and was now mouthing Ernie's, where they were supposed to meet Callie the next day. "Tomorrow would be fine. My brother won't be able to make it. But I think I can help you by myself."

"I'm sure you can," Lisa said warmly. "What time can we meet?"

"I have an early day tomorrow. How about in the afternoon?" asked Joe.

"Fine," said Lisa. "I've got plenty to keep me busy during the morning."

"You know," Joe said, "I think we have a lot in common."

"I agree," Lisa said. "I'm really looking forward to getting together. I'm at the Bayport Inn. What do you say we meet in the coffee shop here at two o'clock?"

"Great," said Joe.

"Okay, then," Lisa replied. "Bye for now."

"What's the idea?" Frank demanded after Joe hung up the phone. "You know we have to see Callie tomorrow."

"*You* have to see Callie," Joe said. "*I've* got a more interesting date."

"You don't know anything about Lisa," Frank said, pointing out the obvious. "You told her an awful lot, and we don't know what her connection is to all this, if she *is* involved. Now you're ready to drop everything and rush to her side. Don't you see that you're taking a risk?"

"No," said Joe flatly. "I see a gorgeous girl, alone in a strange town, maybe in big trouble. Since when have you worried about taking risks? You're so wrapped up in protecting Callie, you won't look out for anyone else."

His face slowly turned red as Frank stared at him. "Look, I didn't mean that. It's just that I get the feeling that Lisa needs us as much as Callie does." He grinned. "*And* she treats me a whole lot better."

Frank shrugged. "All right," he said. "Do what you have to."

The next afternoon at Ernie's, when Frank told Callie that Joe had other plans, Callie seemed indifferent. "That's okay with me," she said. "I'm sure the two of us will function perfectly well without him."

"Well, I miss Joe," said Frank. "I'm so used to having him around. We've been through a lot together. Joe can be a pain in the neck sometimes, but he can also be a lifesaver."

"We'll call him in if we need him," said Callie. "Right now, we need to put together the pieces of this puzzle. And I've come up with a key piece."

"Right. What did you discover?" asked Frank, leaning forward eagerly.

"As I told you over the phone," said Callie, "I went over every move I made yesterday, trying to figure out how that black book got into my bag. Then I remembered. It was yesterday, when I went to City Hall during lunchtime to get my application for a driver's license. I had just gotten it, and was looking it over as I walked down a corridor, when I bumped right into a mailman."

She shrugged. "I guess it was my fault, since I wasn't paying attention. But the mailman had to be walking real fast. He really hit me hard. I dropped my bag, and his mail sack went flying. Everything scattered all over the floor. I remember, he seemed mad. He didn't even look at me. He just started stuffing the letters and parcels back into his bag, even though I tried to apologize. Then I got angry, too. So I stuffed my things back into my bag as fast as I could and stalked off while he was still on his hands and knees scooping up mail. That was when the black book got into my bag. I must have picked it up with my other stuff. I was in such a rush to get out of there, I didn't look carefully at anything."

"Sounds like a possibility," Frank said, nodding.

"More than a possibility," said Callie. "I'm absolutely sure of it. There's no other way that book could have gotten into my bag."

"Then the next step is to find that mailman," said Frank. "What did he look like?"

51

"Let's see," said Callie as she bit into a slice of pizza. "It's not so easy to remember somebody who wouldn't look at you." Then her face brightened. "I remember one thing. He had a beard. A dark beard. And dark sunglasses."

"We can check at the post office," said Frank, "and find out who has that route. So far, so good. Now the next puzzle piece. The code."

"I haven't had much luck," Callie admitted. "I tried to work on it last night, but my mom saw my light on and ordered me to put it out. Honestly, my parents treat me like an adult most of the time, but when push comes to shove, they still act like I'm about seven years old."

"Kids may stop being kids, but parents never stop being parents," Frank said with a grin. "But don't worry too much about the code. I'll just run the entries through the computer, and we'll figure them out in no time."

"Just give me one more crack at it," said Callie. She reached into her shoulder bag and pulled out the piece of paper with the entries. Spreading it out on the table, she stared at it. "The solution seems close."

Frank and Callie were so engrossed in Callie's notes that they didn't realize Chet Morton had approached them until he spoke.

"Hey, no studying in here," Chet said. "You'll ruin everyone's appetite."

"No danger in doing that to you, Chet," Callie

said, grinning. "How can you carry all that food, much less eat it?"

In one hand Chet was holding a large pizza. In the other hand he was balancing three large drinks in plastic glasses.

"No trick at all. I've had years of practice," Chet said. "Do you guys mind if I sit down and join you?"

But before Chet got a chance to sit, a busboy with a loaded tray tried to squeeze by him. He almost made it—*almost*. A corner of the busboy's tray hit Chet's elbow right on his funny bone. His arm jerked and the three plastic glasses flew into the air. Soda spattered down like a sudden thunderstorm. There was no thunder, only Callie's horrified yell.

"Sorry," Chet said, looking down at the damage. "Did I wreck your homework or something?"

"Or something," Callie said as she stared at the illegible ink-streaked paper in front of her. "Yeah, you might say you wrecked something."

Across town, Joe was suffering a setback of his own.

It's your own fault, he told himself. You shouldn't have been in such a hurry to get here. Now he wished he'd played it cooler. He was five minutes early for his appointment with Lisa, stuck waiting for her at a table in the Bayport Inn coffee shop. It definitely would have been better to have made *her* wait. Not long, of course. Just long enough for her to be eager for him to arrive.

Fifteen minutes later Joe had finished his cup of coffee. He was no longer worried about what kind of impression he would make on Lisa. He was worried if he would get to make any impression at all.

And ten minutes after that, he decided that the best thing he could do would be to leave. He'd call her up later and tell her he hadn't been able to show up. He'd apologize in a nice way and set up another date. He'd get up and walk straight out of there—in five minutes, he decided.

Fifteen minutes later—when Lisa was almost forty minutes late for their appointment—Joe finally got up from the table, paid the cashier, and left the coffee shop. He intended to stalk angrily out of the inn, but his feet had ideas of their own.

He found himself approaching the clerk at the reception desk in the lobby. "Excuse me," he said. "Did Lisa, er, Miss Cantwell leave a message for Mr. Hardy?"

The clerk checked his message book and shook his head. "No, she didn't."

"Oh," said Joe and started to turn away. Then he turned back to the clerk. "Is Miss Cantwell in her room? She's late for an appointment with me."

"Maybe," said the clerk. "She stopped here a couple of hours ago to check for messages, then went up to her room. I haven't seen her go out since then."

"I'd like to call her room," said Joe. "Maybe she took a nap and overslept."

"Right," said the clerk. "I'll ring her." He entered Lisa's name into a computer and glanced at the information that flashed up on the monitor. "That's room twenty-two." He picked up a phone, punched in the number, and handed the receiver to Joe.

Joe listened as the phone rang and rang. No one was answering—Lisa wasn't there. Joe Hardy had been stood up.

He slammed down the receiver, and the desk clerk looked at him coldly.

"Miss Cantwell doesn't seem to be in her room, sir. Would you like to leave a message?"

"No thanks," Joe answered. He left the lobby, his hands buried deep in his pockets. It seemed as though Lisa hadn't wanted to keep their date, and that was that.

As Joe approached the parking lot where the van was parked, an uneasy feeling settled in his stomach. It just didn't make sense, he thought. Lisa had acted so friendly the night before. Her not showing up seemed completely out of character. Abruptly he turned and headed back toward the van. What if something had happened to her? There was no way he was leaving before he found out what was going on with Lisa.

He looked around the grounds for a way to get back into the inn and up to Lisa's room. The main entrance was out. The clerk had a clear view of the revolving door.

The inn was a white-shingled building, five stories high, surrounded by a well-tended lawn and flower beds ablaze with purple, yellow, and orange autumn flowers.

His eyes rested on a ladder leaning against the side of the building. It had obviously been used by painters, since there were several large cans of paint on the ground.

Joe noticed that the ladder was extended to reach to the second floor. Near the end of a row of windows, one of them had been left open. Drapes were billowing in the breeze. Joe was in luck—he could duck in there and then out the door to check on room twenty-two.

After looking to make sure that no one was watching him, Joe dragged the ladder over to the open window and climbed two rungs at a time. He was worried that something had happened to Lisa, and he knew he had to go for it.

He flung himself through the open window and prayed there was no one inside to sound an alarm.

His prayer was answered.

There was no one to make a sound when he entered the room.

But there was someone there.

Someone lying face down on the carpeted floor.

Someone he recognized instantly.

"Lisa," he gasped, a sick feeling going through him as he looked at her. She lay there, as still as death.

Chapter 7

GRITTING HIS TEETH, Joe reached for Lisa's wrist. Her hand was limp as he felt for her pulse. He closed his eyes for a moment, sighing with relief. He could feel the pulse, beating steadily.

Gently, he turned her over on her back.

He clenched his fists when he saw the bruise marks on her neck. He wanted to get his hands on the guy who had tried to strangle her.

But he had more important things to do then. He went into the bathroom and soaked a washcloth with cold water. When he returned, he pressed it on her forehead and cheeks.

Finally her eyelids twitched, then fluttered open.

"What—? Where—?" she mumbled until her eyes focused on the face peering down at her. "Joe! What are you doing here?"

"First, tell me what you were doing on the floor," said Joe as he helped her get to her feet.

"I was getting ready to go down to meet you when there was a knock on the door," Lisa said. "If this were New York City, I might have been more cautious. But aside from the neighborhood mugger I met last night, Bayport seems like a safe place. I didn't think twice about opening the door when the guy said he was an electrician checking the wiring. The moment it was open a crack, he forced himself in. The next thing I knew his hands were squeezing my throat and I blacked out."

"Did you get a good look at him?" asked Joe.

Lisa shook her head. "He was wearing a black stocking mask."

"Sounds familiar," said Joe. "In fact, it sounds like an instant replay of what happened to Callie." He looked around the room. Drawers had been pulled out of a desk and a bureau, and clothes were yanked off hangers and strewn around the floor.

"If he didn't fit the description of the mugger who went after Callie, too, I'd say it was just a robbery. But we have to figure it was more than that."

"No doubt about it—especially considering what he said to me," said Lisa.

"He told you something?" said Joe.

"Just 'Stop sniffing around—or you'll stop breathing.' He made sure I heard that before he

59

made me black out," said Lisa, wincing at the memory.

She glanced around her littered room. "Seems like he was looking around for any notes I might have taken. He didn't find anything, though, because I still haven't written anything." She shook her head. "I just don't see how anything ties in with anything else."

"I'm beginning to think that black book Callie had must be the key," Joe said. "It's a good thing she was so gung-ho to break the code. In fact, she or my brother may have done it already."

"Then she's in danger, even more now than before," Lisa said. "Maybe your brother, too. Before we do anything else, we'd better warn them that this guy is still on the prowl and playing rough."

"Maybe they're still at Ernie's," said Joe. "That's a pizza place where they were meeting after school."

"We can take a cab," said Lisa, grabbing a silk scarf and putting it around her throat to hide the bruises. "Feminine vanity," she said with a smile.

Joe grinned back. Then he said, "No need for a cab. I've got my van in the parking lot—if you don't mind the interior. Sometimes I give the guys on the football team a lift—and people have told me that there's a certain atmosphere that lingers."

Lisa grimaced. "It's a good thing I like athletes. Let's go. I just hope we're in time."

When Joe and Lisa arrived at Ernie's, Frank and Callie were still sitting in a booth, staring at the indecipherable remains of Callie's notes and trying to think—without success—of what to do next.

After Lisa and Callie were introduced and the attack on Lisa was described, Frank gave Joe and Lisa the bad news about what had happened to Callie's notes.

"Poor Chet," Callie added. "He couldn't even eat his pizza afterward. He just left it and went home."

"A total disaster, huh?" said Lisa, looking at the remains of the piece of paper. "Can't you dry it out or something?"

"I don't think there's any use trying," said Callie. "The ink is completely smeared."

"Well, there goes our last link to the mugger. We have nothing to track him down with—and he has no reason to go after Callie anymore." Frank glanced around. "I hope."

"It's a tough break," said Lisa sympathetically. "Does this mean you're giving up?"

Callie's voice was indignant. "Not on your life. We'll get that guy yet. And we do know that he's somehow connected to the mailman I bumped into yesterday." Callie quickly explained her theory about how the black book had gotten in her bag to Lisa and Joe.

"If I can do anything to help, let me know," Lisa said.

"Sure. Thanks." Joe smiled eagerly. "That's a great idea. Welcome to the team."

"Don't forget, I'm interested in this case, too. That guy has gone after me twice now," Lisa said.

"That's right—and there has to be a connection," said Frank. "You and Callie must have something in common that we don't know about."

Joe recognized the gleam in his brother's eyes.

"Stand back," Joe said with a grin. "You're about to see my brother's famous brain go into action."

It took just under a minute for Frank to nod to himself.

"I think I've got it," he said, and the others leaned forward. "Callie picked up the black book at City Hall yesterday just about the time that the city manager committed suicide. And Lisa came into town to investigate any scandal that might surround that suicide. Somebody out there doesn't want his connection to the suicide known."

Lisa nodded. "That makes sense."

Joe said, "Now you see how Frank and I operate. He's the brains, I'm the muscles."

"All the way up to and including your head," Callie said. The show that Joe was putting on for Lisa's benefit was simply too much.

"Come on you two," said Frank. "We've got better ways to spend our time right now." Then he asked Lisa, "Did anyone know you were in town to investigate the suicide?"

"I don't think so," she began, then stopped herself and said, "Yes. I did stop by police head-quarters to see if there were any new developments, and I told them I was working on an article."

"Then somebody in the police department could have . . ." Frank let his voice trail off, not wanting to complete the thought out loud.

But Lisa didn't hesitate. "If we *are* on to a case of civic corruption, some of the members of the police force might be involved." She bit her lip. "That means we'll have to conduct this investigation on our own. We can't afford to risk a leak to our mugger."

"Lisa's right," said Joe. "Anyway, Chief Collig would never buy a story like ours, especially since we don't have any hard evidence."

"Yeah," said Frank. "Too bad Riley's away. He would be helpful. But are we agreed that once we do get hard evidence, we turn it over to the authorities?"

The other three nodded.

"The only trouble now is that we can't ask the

63

police for any news about the suicide," said Callie. Then she said, "But we do have one good source of information."

"Who's that?" asked Lisa.

"Liz," said Callie. "Liz Webling. Her father is the editor of the Bayport *Times*. She works there after school, and she always gets the latest news before it's printed."

"But can you trust her to keep quiet?" Lisa asked.

"She's my best friend," said Callie. "All I have to do is explain the situation. She'll be glad to help. I'll give her a call right now."

"I don't know about this," said Joe after Callie crossed the room to make the call. "You know how some girls like to talk. Can we really trust Liz?"

"Trust Callie," said Frank quietly, and everyone fell silent, waiting for her to return.

When Callie turned around to return to them a few minutes later, a worried look crossed Frank's face. "She looks like she found something out— and I think it wasn't good."

"What happened?" asked Lisa when Callie sat down again. "You look like you saw a ghost."

"I heard something more scary than that," said Callie. She took a sip of her drink before continuing. "It seems the cause of Jack Morrison's death has been changed. They did an autopsy, which everyone thought was going to be routine, considering the bullet wound in his head. But a lab assistant noticed a tiny puncture mark on the arm. When they checked it out, they discovered traces of poison. A poison that kills instantly. After more lab tests, the coroner realized that Morrison must have already been dead when the bullet entered him. Jack Morrison's death wasn't a suicide. Someone poisoned him, then staged the suicide."

"But who could have managed to sneak in and out of Mr. Morrison's office in broad daylight?" asked Lisa.

"Well, there's more," Callie said, looking paler than ever. "Morrison's secretary said that the last person who entered and left Morrison's office that day was a mailman—a mailman carrying a registered envelope, which required Morrison's signature." Callie swallowed before continuing. "The mailman had a beard."

"The mailman you bumped into," said Frank.

"The mailman who had the black book," said Joe.

"The mugger who's after us," said Lisa.

"No. He's not just a *mugger* anymore," said Callie. Despite herself, her voice trembled. "The *killer* who's after us."

Chapter

8

THIS TIME CALLIE didn't protest when Frank suggested she needed protection.

"I may be independent—but I'm not stupid," she said. "With a killer shadowing me, I'll take any help I can get, from man, woman, or child." She grinned. "Even from Joe."

"Too bad, Callie, you're out of luck," said Joe. "Lisa needs protection, too."

Lisa flashed him a warm smile. "Thanks, Joe. I didn't want to ask. But I will feel safer with you around."

"I guess I'll have to settle for what's left," Callie said, smiling at Frank. "Think you can handle it?" she asked.

"No sweat." Frank grinned back.

Then he grew serious. "Now that we've got that settled, there's still one little problem." He paused and shook his head. "Without the black book, and without knowing anything about who the killer is, what do we do now?"

"I know what I'm going to do," said Lisa. "Just what I planned—investigate possible city government corruption." She smiled. "A murder makes the story that much more juicy."

"It also makes it that much more dangerous," said Joe. "I'm sticking close to you."

"As close as you want." Lisa grinned.

"Maybe that's the best way," said Frank to himself.

"The best way to do what?" asked Callie. She could practically hear the wheels spinning in Frank's head.

"Maybe investigating possible corruption is the best way to get a lead on the killer." Frank nodded thoughtfully. "If anybody was up to no good and Morrison got wind of it, they'd want to get rid of him. It's worth checking out."

"Then the sooner I get started, the better," said Lisa. She turned to Callie. "Maybe you can help me take the first step."

"Of course," said Callie. "What can I do?"

"You said a friend of yours, Liz, works for the local newspaper," said Lisa. "I'd like to check their back-issue file."

"What are you looking for?" asked Frank. He was gaining more and more respect for Lisa. Trust Joe's instincts next time, he told himself.

"Civic corruption means money," Lisa said. "Money that the city pays out to get work done. I want to check the contracts the city awarded over the past year or so. Maybe I can spot something that looks suspicious. Then I can go check those companies."

Callie was already on her feet. "I'll call Liz right now."

A few minutes later she was back. "Liz is glad to help," Callie reported. "We can meet her at the newspaper in ten minutes."

"Let's go," said Joe. "The van's parked right outside."

Liz was waiting for them at the reception desk when they arrived at the Bayport *Times* office.

When Frank asked her to keep their investigation absolutely confidential, she said impatiently, "Don't worry. I'm a reporter. I know how to keep a secret."

The day's final edition had already been printed and loaded into the delivery trucks. Only a skeleton staff was in the office. Nobody even looked up as Liz led them to the newspaper morgue, the room where back issues were filed.

"You can go through the actual issues, if you want to divide the work. We also have microfilm, but there's only one machine. Before you start, I'll give you some news you won't find here," Liz said. "It'll be in tomorrow's paper."

"What's that?" asked Callie.

"It turns out that Jack Morrison was being secretly investigated for accepting bribes," said Liz. "That's why the police never suspected that his death wasn't a suicide. They figured he had found out that the net was closing in and he didn't want to face the music."

"That also could mean that somebody else found out—and silenced Morrison before he could talk," said Frank.

Liz nodded. "And right now the only clue to that person's identity is a very convincing mailman disguise."

"Let's get at those back issues," said Lisa. "I smell a story. Where do you list city contract awards, Liz?"

"On the back pages—most readers aren't very interested in them," said Liz. "That's been one of my assignments this past year—going down to City Hall for that information. It's the kind of boring job that nobody else wants. Oh, well, I have to start someplace."

"You might save us some time," said Frank. "Were any big contracts handed out lately?"

"There have been so many, and it's such a routine process. It's hard to think of any that stand out," said Liz, her brows knitting. Then she said, "But I do remember one—maybe because it affected me directly."

"Which one?" asked Callie.

"The food-catering contract for Bayport High School," said Liz. "It was awarded just last summer, to start this fall term."

"So that's why," said Callie, grimacing.

"Why—what?" asked Lisa.

"Why the food in the cafeteria has been the way it is," said Callie.

"Which is?" Lisa persisted.

"Let's just say that if I fed it to my dog, he'd stop being my best friend fast," she answered. "The only kids in school who like it are the girls on diets. One bite and you not only stop eating, your appetite is killed for hours."

"Yeah," Joe added with a grin. "Even Chet Morton won't go back for seconds."

"Sounds like the kind of thing we're after," said Lisa. "What's the name of the outfit?"

Liz had flipped through the files to find it. "Eat-Right, Inc. Five ninety-seven Elm Street."

"The rest of you can hunt for other contracts while I check this one out," said Lisa.

"Good idea. A team effort," said Frank.

"Yeah, you three do that," said Joe, "while Lisa and I handle Eat-Right."

"*You* and Lisa?" asked Frank.

"No way she goes to that place alone," said Joe. "If they're capable of doing what they do to food, who knows what they might do to people?"

"Your coming along is a great idea, Joe," Lisa added. "I have the perfect plan: We'll pretend we're reporters from the high school paper, doing a story on the new catering company."

Joe nodded enthusiastically. "Come on, Lisa. We better hurry. They'll close by five-thirty or six."

Fifteen minutes later, when they pulled up in front of the Bayport Inn, Lisa said, "Wait for me in the lobby. I'll be down in a half-hour."

Lisa was better than her word. Twenty-five minutes later she stepped out of an elevator.

But it took Joe two minutes to recognize her.

Her hair was black with purple streaks, and it looked even shorter than it had before. She wore an oversize black cotton sweatsuit and high-top black aerobic sneakers. Her eyelids were caked with green eyeshadow. Lisa looked about seventeen years old.

"How did you do it?" asked Joe. "I thought you were a reporter, not an actress."

"Sometimes I have to be both," explained Lisa. "I used this wig and outfit when I did a story about bars and clubs serving liquor to minors. Sometimes people tell teenagers things they won't tell adults. How about it? Do you think I look like a real reporter from Bayport High?"

"You could fool me," said Joe. "Of course, you don't look that old to begin with."

"Funny, I think the same thing about you, but

71

in reverse," said Lisa. "I mean, it's hard to think of you as a teenager. You seem so grownup."

Her eyes met his. Joe felt warm, as if the heat had suddenly gone up in the hotel lobby.

Then Lisa's cool voice brought him back to the business at hand. "But we both have to be teenagers now. Two kids from the high school paper doing a story on the nice folks who provide those delicious cafeteria lunches."

Eat-Right, Inc. was housed in a grimy, factory-like building down the street from the town incinerator. The odor of refuse hung in the air.

"Yuck," said Joe, his nose wrinkling. "Now I know where they get the garbage they serve at school."

They stood in front of a door with a sign that read: "Welcome to the Offices of Eat-Right, Inc. A Name That Guarantees Dining Delight."

"Let's check it out," said Lisa, opening the door. Joe was close behind her, alert for any sign of trouble.

Eat-Right, Inc. certainly seemed like a legitimate business. When Lisa explained why they were there, the receptionist flashed them a warm smile, picked up her phone, and relayed the information to the person at the other end. Then she nodded, hung up, and said in a smooth voice, "Mr. Smith of public relations hasn't left for the day yet. He has a few minutes and will be out to answer your questions. Maybe next time it would be better to make an appointment. But please do sit down and make yourselves comfortable as long as you're here."

Lisa and Joe sat down in soft leather chairs in the tastefully decorated reception room. Joe picked up one of the gourmet magazines arranged on a table and thumbed through it. He had just started an article entitled "Twenty Ways to Stuff a Lobster" when Mr. Smith appeared.

Mr. Smith was a pleasant-looking man in his thirties. He wore a gray three-piece suit, highly polished black shoes, a striped tie, and a spotless white shirt.

"Always glad to help young people," he assured Lisa and Joe. "This is a splendid idea, doing an article on our company. The way we prepare food here will give students valuable insights into the latest advances in nutrition and preparation. Real food for thought." He chuckled and repeated, "Food for thought. A little joke."

Real little, thought Joe, forcing himself to chuckle when he saw Lisa doing it. He definitely had to respect her. She was a pro.

Still smiling, Mr. Smith led them through a door, down a corridor, and into a fully equipped laboratory. A tall man in a white lab coat looked up from a microscope when they entered.

"This is Dr. Purvis," said Mr. Smith. "The doctor checks food samples and does nutritional

73

research to upgrade our menus. Right, doctor?"

"That's right," said Dr. Purvis. "Let me show you something I think you'll find interesting." He lead them to a cage filled with white mice. "A few weeks ago these mice were practically dead. Now see how healthy and active they've become—just by improving their diet."

Joe and Lisa nodded politely as they looked at the mice in the cage.

"Well, we don't want to take up any more of your valuable time, doctor. Keep up the good work," said Mr. Smith. "Now to the food itself."

He led Joe and Lisa down the corridor and into another room, which was much larger than the lab. Workers in white smocks, with white caps on their heads, white surgical masks on their faces, and rubber gloves on their hands, were just finishing up the food preparation for the next day.

"As you can see, no expense has been spared to insure absolute cleanliness," Mr. Smith said as he pointed out the gleaming stainless-steel urns and large microwave ovens. "Now button up your coats and take a look at this."

He opened a steel door and led them into a walk-in freezer. Sides of meat had been hung on wall hooks, and crates of frozen poultry were piled on the floor.

"Everything is government inspected—Grade A," said Mr. Smith, his breath forming clouds of frozen moisture in the air.

"Very impressive," said Lisa, peeking in.

Back in the corridor, Mr. Smith said, "I'm sorry I don't have any vegetables to show you, but we get them delivered fresh every morning, and, of course, we've already used up today's shipment. Anyway, I hope you've seen enough to know that Eat-Right is dedicated to giving you food that tastes the very best and is the best for you."

"We sure have," Lisa said. "One more thing. May we interview the company's president? We'd like our readers to know how Eat-Right started . . . how the president got into this business."

"I'm sorry, but Mr. Karnovsky has already left," said Mr. Smith. "If you'd like, I'll send you a brief biography just as soon as I can have one typed up. And now if there's nothing else, I'm afraid it really is closing time."

"Can't think of anything," said Lisa. "Thank you very much, Mr. Smith."

"Thank *you*," Mr. Smith said as he ushered them out.

"PR people—they're all the same," Lisa said to Joe as they stood outside on the sidewalk.

"He was pretty good," said Joe. "He might have convinced me if I hadn't actually tasted the food."

"He's just a front," said Lisa. "It's what's going on behind the closed doors here at Eat-

Right that we're interested in. Come on, before anyone spots us still hanging around.''

As she spoke, the lights in the building began to go out. In a minute the staff would be leaving. Lisa headed around to the back of the building.

"Here's where they take deliveries," said Joe as they crouched beside a concrete loading platform. In the deepening darkness the platform was illuminated only by a dim red light. "What now?"

"We wait," said Lisa.

Fifteen minutes later a pickup truck quietly rolled up to the platform. Its headlights were turned off. Men suddenly walked out of the building. As the door opened and shut, Lisa and Joe could see that the interior of the building was brightly lit.

"They have the back windows blacked out," Joe whispered.

The men were unloading crates from the truck and piling them on the platform. As soon as it was emptied, the truck drove off.

"Let's take a break before we haul this last load inside," said one of the men. The others agreed, and there was a flash of light as they entered the building before closing the door again.

"Now's our chance," said Lisa, hoisting herself onto the platform. Joe was right behind her.

They reached the crates. Joe stuck his hand inside one between the slats, and said, "Ugh."

He withdrew his hand, which was dripping with the remains of a mushy tomato. He sniffed it, and repeated, "Ugh. This must be a month old."

"So much for their fresh vegetables every day," said Lisa. She moved to another crate. "Let's see what's inside this one."

Before she could open it, Joe grabbed her arm. The door to the building was opening. The workers were coming back outside.

He yanked Lisa to the edge of the platform, and they dove off it. Joe felt his palm smash against the asphalt below, then his knees hit. He reacted just as he did on the football field—relaxing his body to roll with the impact. Instantly he turned in Lisa's direction.

"You okay?" he whispered as loud as he dared.

"Yeah," she said. "But we were too slow. They spotted us."

Flashlight beams cut through the darkness.

Joe grabbed Lisa's hand and started to run. Good thing Lisa had run track in college, he thought grimly. Her speed was about to come in handy.

"Oh, no," she said. They skidded to a stop.

Moving directly at them was a truck.

"Another delivery," gasped Lisa.

Her voice was drowned out by a man on the platform shouting, "Prowlers! Stop them!"

The truck driver flicked on his headlights, and Lisa and Joe were caught in their glare.

Lisa wheeled around to run in the other direction. But Joe had already seen the door by the driver's seat opening and a man leaping out. And in his hand—

"Duck," Joe said. "He's got a gun!"

His warning came too late.

There was a sharp cracking noise. Lisa gave a cry, stiffened, and fell. Joe's gut twisted. *No,* he thought.

The man with the gun raised his hand again.

Run—*fast,* a voice inside Joe's head cried, but he couldn't make himself move.

Another crack—and Joe felt the pain.

This time I've bought it. He swayed on his feet. Then the darkness closed in.

Chapter

9

"I WONDER WHAT'S keeping them," Frank said to Callie. "I'm getting worried."

"It *is* getting late," said Callie. She looked at her watch. "Seven o'clock."

They sat in the Hardys' living room. Callie had already called her parents to say she wouldn't be home for dinner. She and Frank had said goodbye to Liz at the newspaper office after compiling a list of contracts awarded by the city over the past year. Then they had gone back to the Hardys' to wait for Joe and Lisa.

"Maybe they went back to the Bayport Inn," Frank said. "I'll call Lisa's room."

He made the call, then hung up. He shook his head and said, "Lisa's not in. Actually, the guy at the switchboard was surprised by that. It seems he saw her go back to the inn a couple of hours before with Joe, but he didn't see her leave. He did see Joe leave, but with another girl. Some teenager."

"He probably ran into her at the inn and asked her out on the spot," Callie said.

"Not likely," said Frank, "from the look in Joe's eyes when he gazes at Lisa. It's more likely that Lisa made herself look younger so that their cover as reporters would be more believable."

"You're probably right. That sounds like Lisa's style. She's pretty amazing," said Callie thoughtfully. "I haven't seen Joe this interested in any girl since—well, in a long time." She looked at Frank. "Well, let's get moving. You don't have to tell me what we have to do now. I can figure that out for myself. We go to Eat-Right and pick up their trail."

"You took the words right out of my mouth," said Frank, putting on his coat.

They took a bus that dropped them off two blocks from Eat-Right. They walked the distance quickly. Then they stood and stared at the darkened building.

"Looks like everybody's gone home."

"Yeah," said Frank. "It sure looks deserted." He ran his hand through his hair. "Something feels wrong, though. If they're not in trouble, we should have heard from them by now." He

80

' turned to Callie. "Let's check this place out, anyway."

Just then they heard a sound from behind the building.

"That's a car starting," said Frank. "Quick. Get out of sight."

Frank and Callie pressed themselves against the building. A moment later a van moved out from behind the building and sped off. As it passed under a streetlight Frank and Callie got a look at the lettering on the side panel.

"What on earth could a dog-food company want here?" wondered Callie.

"I don't even want to think about that," said Frank. "Let's find out what's going on."

They moved swiftly to the loading platform around the back and stood facing darkened windows.

Frank stepped up to the windows and pointed his pen flashlight at one of the panes. "The glass is painted black," he said. "Somebody doesn't want anyone looking inside."

He tried the door, but it was locked.

While Callie looked on wide-eyed, Frank took out a Swiss army knife. At least it looked like a Swiss army knife. But it contained a metal pick that was definitely not Swiss army standard equipment.

"My dad gave one of these to Joe and me, and showed us how to use them," he explained as he went to work on the lock. "He said if we were going to fool around with detective work, we should have the tools of the trade."

When he heard the tumblers click, he withdrew the pick and opened the door a crack.

Cautiously, he peered inside.

"Oh!" he gasped.

There, lying side by side on the floor in the middle of the room, were two bodies. Joe and a young girl with black hair streaked with purple.

Frank reached them first and kneeled down beside them. At closer range he recognized Lisa. "Lisa did disguise herself," he remarked grimly.

Then he swiftly felt their wrists. He looked up at Callie, who was trembling, all color drained from her face.

"They're alive," he said, and Callie felt her heart begin to beat again. "But they're out cold."

Callie dampened her scarf at the water cooler and pressed it against Joe's forehead, then Lisa's.

Joe was the first to show signs of life. His body twitched and he groaned softly. "What happened?"

Then Lisa began to stir. She rubbed her shoulder. "Ouch," she said. "Something stung me."

Joe's hand went to his thigh. "Me, too."

Then a voice came from an open doorway, making the foursome look up.

"*This* gun doesn't have darts in it, kids. It has bullets. They don't sting—they kill."

A tall man in a white lab coat was standing in the doorway. His coat was spotted with reddish brown stains. Only one substance dried to that unmistakable color—blood. And in the man's hand was a gleaming, nickel-plated .45.

"Dr. Purvis," Joe gasped.

"I think we can forget the 'doctor,' " said Lisa. "And probably the 'Purvis,' too."

"Smart kids," said the man. "There are four of you now, I see. What is this, some kind of class project? Follow me. Let's see what the boss wants to do with you."

The phony doctor herded the four of them down a hallway lit by fluorescent lights. He stopped outside a door marked President and knocked loudly. "It's Rocky. With some visitors."

"Come in," said a voice with a strong French accent.

Rocky pushed open the door and ushered his prisoners in.

The man behind the desk in the center of the office was holding a thin slice of toast heaped with glistening caviar. He looked at his visitors, put down the caviar, and belched loudly.

"All this excitement when I am eating," he complained. "It is so bad for the digestion."

He reached for a glass filled with bubbling champagne and took a sip.

"There, that is better," he said, his tongue

circling over his thick lips to catch the traces of champagne. Then he stood up, patting his huge stomach.

The president of Eat-Right looked like a living advertisement for the joy of eating. He had a blimplike body that his expensively tailored pin-striped suit could not begin to disguise. A roll of pink flesh bulged over the collar of his wide-striped silk shirt. Only dining well and often for years could have produced the man who now introduced himself as Jacques Karnovsky.

"And you kids, who are you?" he demanded.

"These two are the high school reporters that we caught snooping out back," said Rocky, indicating Joe and Lisa. "I just caught the other two coming to rescue them."

"Look, I apologize for butting in here," said Joe. "I can see how you might have thought we were thieves and all. But, honest, we were just curious about Eat-Right. I guess we shouldn't have been. I mean, we haven't found anything wrong with your operation. And if you just let us go, we'll forget about the whole thing."

"How much did they see?" Karnovsky asked Rocky.

"They must have gotten a good look at the vegetables that came in tonight," said Rocky. "And they could have gotten a look at the meat delivery."

"Good thing the driver had the dart gun

handy," said Karnovsky. "Otherwise they would have gotten away."

That was all the information it took for Frank to put two and two together. The answer he came up with made his stomach lurch.

"Did you say dart gun?" he asked to make sure, hoping he was wrong. "Is that what you used on Lisa and Joe?"

"Should I tell him?" Rocky asked his boss.

"Why not?" said Karnovsky shoving the toast and caviar into his mouth. With his mouth full, he added, "They are not going to pass on the information. We will make sure of that."

"Our meat supplier sometimes needs a dart gun to knock out misbehaving animals," said Rocky. "You know, when horses get sick—" He grinned. "The driver's real good with it. Two shots, and the two of you went down like bowling pins."

"Your meat supplier shot us? And he shoots sick horses?" Joe stared blankly. Then he understood. "No, you've got to be kidding."

"Oh, he's not kidding," Frank said, assuring him he was right. "Callie and I saw a van driving away from here—a van from a dog-food company."

"It must have just finished unloading its, um, delivery," said Callie.

"You know, I just thought of something," said Joe. "That meat loaf that the cafeteria serves."

"What about the hamburgers?" asked Frank.

"And the veal goulash," said Callie. She swallowed hard. "Know what? I've just become a vegetarian."

"But that's impossible to even consider," said Lisa. "You don't mean—you don't actually—"

"Americans—you can feed them anything," Karnovsky answered her question, his mouth wrinkling with distaste. "Even the meat that dog-food companies won't touch. When I first came to this country from France, I dreamed of running a fine restaurant. But then I saw my customers putting catsup on my greatest creations, and demanding a revolting orange-colored fluid to put on my beautiful salads. I decided there is only one way to make a fortune here. I must give Americans the kind of food they want and deserve."

"This is too much talk and not enough action," said Rocky. "We've got to figure out what to do with these kids. They blab, and we're washed up."

"We may be washed up, anyway," said Karnovsky thoughtfully as he spooned more caviar onto toast. "Now that Morrison has committed suicide, we cannot be sure we can make an arrangement with whoever takes his job. Perhaps we will have to move our business to another city. Pity. Things were running so smoothly here."

"And these kids?" Rocky asked again.

Karnovsky looked them up and down. "They all seem prime specimens. Good solid meat on their bones."

"Hey, Karnovsky," said Joe. "Did anybody ever tell you that you have a real sick sense of humor?"

But Karnovsky wasn't smiling.

Rocky wasn't smiling, either.

As the two men stood face-to-face, Frank and Joe exchanged glances. They both saw their chance—and took it.

Joe dived at Rocky, grabbing the arm that held the gun.

Wielding a meat cleaver night after night had made Rocky's arm as strong as iron. Joe grabbed it with both hands to keep him from bringing it up. But there was no way to stop Rocky's other hand from smashing into Joe's jaw and sending him sprawling halfway across the room.

Frank barreled into Karnovsky, the top of his head butting into Karnovsky's stomach.

But bashing into Karnovsky was like hitting a brick wall. Karnovsky didn't go down. Frank merely bounced off him, stunned, while Karnovsky moved to his desk to get the gun hidden inside a drawer.

Fortunately, Joe and Frank weren't alone.

Callie was at the desk in an instant. She reached into the open caviar tin and pulled out a handful of gooey caviar—and hit Karnovsky square in the face.

At the same time Lisa went for the champagne bottle. She grabbed it by the neck and smashed it over Rocky's head. He stood tottering and dazed, while the foursome got ready to make a quick exit.

They had reached the corridor when they heard Karnovsky's bellow of rage. "After them! Don't let them get out of here alive!"

"We can make it out the back door," said Frank. But when they reached it, it wouldn't budge.

Frank smacked his forehead with the palm of his hand. "I'm a numbskull. I forgot Rocky re-locked it." He reached for his lock pick.

"There's no time. I hear them coming," said Joe.

"Let's try this way," said Lisa, indicating another door leading out of the room.

The door swung open, and the four of them jumped through it.

They all felt the icy air immediately.

"We're in some kind of freezer," whispered Joe in the darkness.

Outside Karnovsky was yelling. "They can't have gotten out. They're in here somewhere. As soon as you see them, Rocky, shoot to kill."

"I'm free-eezing," whispered Callie through chattering teeth.

"Which would you prefer?" asked Joe.

"Turning to ice in here—or facing the gunfire outside?"

"What's the difference?" said Lisa. "Either way we die."

Chapter
10

OUTSIDE THE WALK-IN freezer, Karnovsky and Rocky exchanged triumphant smiles.

"They've got to be in there," said Rocky. "We're going to have some very cool kids in a couple of minutes."

"Let's check it out right now," said Karnovsky. "We can't afford to let them get away. We're going to need a couple of weeks to clear away all traces of our operation now that Morrison is gone. After that, we can declare bankruptcy and clear out."

"You're the boss," said Rocky, reaching for the door handle.

"Be careful," said Karnovsky. "There are four of them."

"Don't worry. There are eight slugs in one of

these," said Rocky, indicating the .45 in his hand.

"And twenty in this one," said Karnovsky, who had a small but deadly black Italian Beretta. "I'll come in right behind you."

Rocky swung open the door. "Kids, I know you're in here. Come out with your hands up."

"Maybe they're frozen stiff already," said Karnovsky when no one answered.

"It'll be easy to find out," said Rocky, reaching for the light switch.

"Hide-and-seek is over."

He never knew what hit him. Neither did Karnovsky.

The Hardys stood examining their weapons.

"What do you think this is supposed to be, leg of lamb?" asked Joe, tossing his frozen weapon to the floor.

"I don't know—but this leg has a horseshoe at the end," said Frank as he laid his weapon beside it.

"Ugh, I don't want to think about it," said Callie. She dropped the mangy-looking frozen chicken she'd been holding at the ready.

"This sure isn't government-inspected, Grade-A meat like the stuff in the freezer up front," said Lisa, throwing away an unidentifiable animal. "It's real mystery meat."

"Come on, let's get out of here," said Callie. "I don't feel very steady right now."

"I have to admit, I've felt better myself," said

Joe. He and Callie grinned shakily at each other. "Nice of you to admit it," she murmured.

"Come on, then," said Frank, who had found a key ring in Rocky's pocket and was on his way to unlock the back door.

"Wait a second," said Lisa. "We have to figure out what to do with these bozos."

"Easy," said Joe. "We drop them off at the police station. The cops will be real interested in their operation."

"Hold on," said Lisa. "Let's think this through. We're not altogether sure that the police force isn't somehow mixed up in the scandal at City Hall. I think we have to keep the cops out of this until we know more."

"What do you suggest we do?" Frank asked, nodding in agreement.

"Why don't we take them to your house?" asked Lisa. "We can grill them there and find out if anyone else is involved in this mess."

"And also find out if they're the ones who wasted Morrison and grabbed the black book," said Joe.

"I don't think so," Callie said, frowning. "From what Karnovsky said back in the office, he had no idea that Morrison's suicide was a fake. So he couldn't be the one who did the killing and the heist."

"Hey, with you two girls around, I feel like an

extra spoke on a wheel," said Frank. "You're doing all the detective work."

"Oh, don't feel bad," said Callie, grinning. "If you're good we'll let you in on the fun."

Lisa scooped up both guns, putting the Beretta in her shoulder bag and keeping the .45 in her hand. "I'd better take care of these. I've got a gun permit, since my work can take me into some rough neighborhoods."

"That's fine with me," Frank said. "We don't handle guns unless we have to."

Lisa trained the .45 on the two men. "Come on, guys, we're going for a ride."

Karnovsky and Rocky groaned as they climbed to their feet and walked out ahead of Lisa to the Hardys' van.

After a short ride Lisa herded the prisoners into the Hardys' house.

"You handle that gun like a real pro," Joe remarked.

"Glad I *look* convincing," she whispered in his ear so that Karnovsky and Rocky couldn't hear. "I'd hate to think about what would happen if I actually had to use this thing."

But inside the house, even the gun in Lisa's hand couldn't scare the two men into talking.

"I do not know anyone else who is paying off Morrison," Karnovsky maintained. "When the applications for the high school food contract were sent out, I approached Morrison and hinted I would pay him a reasonable amount if Eat-Right got the contract. We met and figured out how much profit I would make. Then he asked for one-fifth of it, and we made the deal. He was very businesslike, a good man to work with. It is a great pity he is gone—especially since whoever replaces him may start nosing around."

"He won't have to look far," said Joe. "Not after we hand you over to the cops."

"In the meantime, we have to figure out what to do with these two," said Frank.

"Is there someplace in the house you can put them?" asked Lisa. "Someplace secure?"

"As a matter of fact, there is," said Joe. "Our dad's new file room."

"Right," Frank said, nodding. Then he explained to the girls, "There was a case awhile ago where some thugs broke into his office to swipe some private information. Afterward, my dad decided he needed better security, so he built a file room in the cellar with reinforced concrete walls and a steel door."

"It sounds perfect," said Lisa.

"You cannot do this—cage us like animals," protested Karnovsky.

"Yeah, we've got our rights," said Rocky.

"Sure you do," said Lisa as she leveled her gun at them. "Like those rejects from the dog-food company. Like us when you were ready to do away with us. I don't want to hear about your rights. It makes me mad."

Joe stared at Lisa. Her tone was brutal. But then she turned and winked at him. She was bluffing. He relaxed.

"Okay, okay, don't get nervous with that thing," Rocky said hastily.

"A gentleman never argues with a lady," said Karnovsky, shrugging.

"Let's head down to the cellar," said Joe after getting the keys to the file room from their hiding place behind a painting.

"How long do you intend to hold us here?" asked Karnovsky.

"As long as we have to," Frank answered.

"I hope you will give us more than bread and water to eat," said Karnovsky. He patted his huge stomach. "Indeed, I am getting hungry already. I am accustomed to regular meals. Five a day."

"We'll figure out something," said Frank.

"I already have," said Joe. "Wait a sec while I go to the kitchen. I'll get you your first night's meal."

A minute later he returned with a stack of cans held in both hands.

Karnovsky nose wrinkled in distaste. "Canned food. I should have known. So very American."

"What do you mean?" Joe said with mock indignation. "I'm giving you a great gourmet selection. My aunt Gertrude buys only the best for when she pet-sits."

"Cat food," said Karnovsky, turning pale as he read the labels.

Joe shrugged. "It's a lot better than what you've been feeding the kids at school."

"Never," said Karnovsky.

"You're sick, kid," Rocky said, glowering.

"And you're going to be mighty hungry in a day or so," said Joe. "I think I'll spoon out a selection of all the varieties on your plate to see which one you eat first. A kind of taste test. My aunt's clients prefer the fish heads, but maybe you'll go for one of the other treats."

After interviewing them a bit longer, the four were convinced that they were not involved with either the muggings or the murder. They'd have to check further.

"We have to look for other people who have made payoffs to Morrison," said Frank. "That's still our only lead to the killer."

"How did your research at the newspaper go?" Lisa asked.

"It went well—too well, in fact," said Frank.

"We came up with a whole bunch of contracts that the city has awarded over the past year, plus building permits and zoning variations," Callie explained. "It's funny, you never think about how much influence politicians have until they're caught being crooked. They sure can influence everyone if they mess up on the job."

"Can I see your list?" asked Lisa. She skimmed the sheets of paper that Callie handed her. "You're right. It is immense. But it's all we have. We'll have to go over it carefully to look for the most suspicious deals, the ones involving the most money. Then we can start investigating them and hope we get lucky."

"Luck is what we need," said Frank. "We can keep those guys locked down there for only so long. Sooner or later someone will wonder where they are. Besides, the family is coming back in a few days. My dad and mom might go along with keeping those two under wraps, but my aunt Gertrude would totally freak out."

"We'll do our best," said Callie. "Frank and I made four copies of the list. We can each study them tonight and meet tomorrow to compare notes and decide on our next move. Meanwhile, I'd better go home. My mom'll be worried enough already."

"I'll walk you home," said Frank. "That mugger is still out there."

"You don't have to," said Lisa. "I'll walk with Callie. She can tell me more about the town on the way, and I'm packing all the protection we need." She patted her shoulder bag. The two guns were in it, and the catch was left open for instant access.

"Okay," said Frank. "Joe and I will start looking over the list as soon as you leave."

"Right," said Joe. "See you tomorrow."

After the two girls left, Joe said to Frank, "I don't want to hurt your feelings, but working on a case with Lisa is something else. Brains, guts, and good looks, too. What more can a guy look for in a partner?"

"Working with Callie isn't so bad, either," said Frank. "She always manages to keep her cool—unlike some hotheads I know."

The Hardys stood in silence for a moment. Then Joe met Frank's eyes. His own expression was carefully neutral.

"Maybe we should keep the setup on this case just like it is," he said. "Two teams are better than one, and all that stuff."

"That's fine with me," said Frank. "Let's get to work on this list."

The Hardys sat side-by-side at the dining room table with one copy of the list in front of them. Each ran his eyes down the sheet of paper, noting all the individuals and corporations who had done business with the city over the past year.

"Hey, here's a live one," said Joe. "Acme Waste Disposal Corporation. They've got a license from the city to remove hazardous wastes from local factories. I've heard that companies like that have ties to organized crime."

"Don't believe everything you hear," said Frank. "Most of them are respectable businesses—doing valuable work. Without them, the environment would be in even worse shape than it is now."

"Well, I'm writing it down," said Joe. "All those stories have to mean something. Where there's smoke—"

"You can't see anything clearly," Frank cut him off. "I want something better than rumor to go on."

"Look, I'll write down the names I want to investigate, and you write down yours," said Joe. "You can't always depend on brain power. Sometimes you have to go with gut feeling."

Frank nodded and went back to studying the list. After fifteen minutes of concentrating, he shook his head. "It doesn't look like it makes any difference what approach we use. With all these names, the only way to come up with suspects is to put the list on the wall and throw darts at it."

Joe glared at the list one more time, then agreed. "You're right. I just hope Lisa has better luck. With her experience as a reporter, she may be able to pick out something that looks fishy."

"Callie may notice something we're missing, too," Frank responded quickly. "Especially with

Liz to help her. Liz knows the city inside out."

Just then they heard a scuffling sound at the front door.

Frank and Joe exchanged looks. They knew what the other was thinking. There was only one person who might be coming to call on them at that time of night.

The man in the black stocking mask. The one who had been stalking them.

Chapter

11

"I'LL CHECK HIM out through the peephole, then swing the door open fast," Frank said. "You stand next to the door and jump him."

"Right," said Joe. "Wait a sec while I get some insurance out of the hall closet."

Joe opened the closet door and pulled out a baseball bat. "Didn't think I'd need this baby again till spring." The doorbell rang again as Joe positioned himself against the wall next to the door. As Frank flipped open the peephole his bat was at the ready.

"Watch out, he's sure to be in disguise," Joe cautioned.

"Yeah, the man with a thousand faces," Frank said as he peered out.

Then he grabbed the door handle and yanked the door open.

At the same time, he shouted to Joe, "Hold it. Don't swing!"

Joe froze, barely able to check his swing. Then his mouth dropped open as he saw the person he'd been about to clobber.

"Lisa," he gasped.

"Help me," she said as she stooped to lift up the limp body fallen beside the door.

It was Frank's turn to gasp. "Oh, no! Not again!" He rushed to help Lisa carry Callie into the house.

"I think she'll be okay," said Lisa. "Her pulse is fine. Nothing seems broken."

Together they laid her gently on the living room couch. Frank stacked pillows under her feet, so that blood would circulate to her brain and speed her return to consciousness.

"What hit her?" asked Frank.

"The same thing that hit me," said Lisa, gingerly touching the back of her neck. "But before I explain, let's tend to Callie."

"I'm one step ahead of you," said Joe, returning from the kitchen with a bowl of ice and a wet dishcloth. "First you this afternoon, now Callie. I'm already a pro at this."

As Joe applied the ice and wet towel to Callie's wrists and forehead, Lisa told the Hardys what happened.

"He must have been hiding behind a tree waiting for us," she said. "I mean, when I first saw Bayport, I thought it was really charming to have a town with streets lined with big old oak trees. I didn't see them as natural spots for ambush. I didn't figure Bayport as a jungle."

"I never have, either," said Frank. "But I'm changing my mind fast." He looked down anxiously at Callie. She stirred slightly, and he breathed more easily. He turned to Lisa. "Sorry. Go on. What happened next?"

"He was as fast as lightning," she said. "He chopped me on the back of the neck and I went down. Then he hit Callie. But he moved too fast for his own good. He didn't hit me squarely. When he turned back to check on me, I was already on my knees, pulling the gun from my bag. He saw the gun, and he turned and ran."

"Great work," said Joe.

Lisa shook her head. "Not so great. I mean, I got the gun out and he was still within range—but I couldn't pull the trigger. I told myself I should, but I couldn't."

"Look, don't feel bad, it's understandable," said Joe sympathetically.

"I guess you're right," said Lisa. "But I'll bet *you* would have."

"Well, anyway, I plan to stick close to you from now on, with that goon still on the loose," promised Joe.

"Thanks, Joe," said Lisa. Their eyes met and locked.

On Frank's face there was a troubled look.

"So this guy got away again?"

"Yes, and no," Lisa answered, turning to face him. "I've given you the bad news; now I'll give you the good."

"You saw who he was," said Joe.

"Not *that* good," said Lisa. "I didn't get a look at his face, just at his back. When my finger froze on the trigger, the only thing I could do was chase him and try to capture him. I followed him down the street. He passed a parked car and I saw him hesitate a second as if he were thinking about getting in. But I was too close. He picked up speed and tore around a corner. By the time I made it to the corner he had disappeared."

She shrugged. "I felt really bad, but I had to hurry back to Callie. As I went by the parked car, though, I remembered how he hesitated so I looked in. In the backseat I saw a suit, and a shirt and tie. It had to be his car. He must have changed out of normal clothes to do his muggings, then back into them when he made his getaway."

"Makes sense," said Frank, nodding.

"Made enough sense for me to take a closer look," said Lisa. "I used the gun to smash the car window, then I reached in and unlocked the door.

If I was wrong, I figured I'd leave some money to cover the damage. But I wasn't. I opened the glove compartment, and—well, look for yourself."

She reached in her shoulder bag and pulled it out.

The black book.

"Let's get to work on it," said Frank eagerly. Then he paused. "But first we should stake out that car. Maybe we can catch the mugger when he returns for it."

Lisa shook her head. "No luck. As soon as I got back to Callie and made sure she wasn't seriously hurt, I went back to the car to do just that. But the guy beat me to it. The car was gone."

"Then this book is all we've got," said Frank. "We'd better make the most of it."

"Let me at it," called a voice from the couch. Callie was sitting up and looking at the black book like a cat at a mouse.

"Hey, take it easy," said Frank with concern. "How do you feel?"

"Lousy," Callie replied. She put a hand to her head. "Listen, we have to catch this guy. I refuse to go through this every day. Oh, I have to call my mom before she gets upset."

"Lie down," Frank told her as he went to dial Mrs. Shaw.

"Don't worry, I'm basically okay," said Callie when he returned. "I'm not going to let a little thing like being knocked out give you a head start on decoding that book—especially since I think I know how to do it."

"What do you mean?" asked Frank.

"I'll show you," said Callie. "Do you have your old American lit textbook handy?"

"Up in my room," said Frank. "But what—?"

"Get it, and I'll show you," said Callie.

"Look, this is no time for a literary discussion," said Joe. "This is a time for Frank's computer and then some fast action."

"Then let's not waste time arguing," Callie said, refusing to be argued with. "I know what I'm doing. Frank, get me that book."

Frank returned with the textbook and Callie flipped swiftly through the pages to find what she wanted.

"Here it is," she announced. "A story by Edgar Allan Poe. 'The Gold Bug.' Poe wrote great detective stories," said Callie. " 'The Gold Bug' is one of them. In it, a detective has to break a code. And Poe describes exactly how to do it."

"But that story is so old," protested Joe.

"What does it matter?" said Callie as she scanned the story to find the passage she wanted. "The basic principles remain the same." Then she leaned forward. "Here's what I'm looking for. First Poe shows the frequency with which certain letters appear in the English language. Then he shows how to use the frequency to break a number code, which is what we have here."

"Partially a number code," Frank said, reminding her. "Each entry also has a small group of letters."

"Right. That *is* a problem," said Callie.

Then Frank's expression brightened. "But if we're talking about a list of payoffs, the letters could represent numbers—the amount of each bribe. Then the numbers would still represent the letters spelling the names of the people doing the bribing."

"All right, Frank." Callie grinned. "Now let's see what Mr. Poe has to say about getting those names."

"How about giving Poe a helping hand—with my computer," said Frank. "I'm sure he wouldn't mind. He had a real interest in artificial intelligence. I read how he once exposed a phony chess-playing robot." He shook his head. "But I can't picture him tapping out 'The Raven' on a word processor."

Joe grimaced at their enthusiasm. "Don't get lost in your fun and games—we still have to translate all this into action."

"How could we forget with you around?" said Frank. "Let's get upstairs and warm up my computer."

It took him twenty minutes to program Poe's code-breaking system into his computer. He tapped the final key and said, "I hope this works. It's not a bad system, but it's not super-sophisticated."

"Neither was Morrison," said Callie. "I'm sure this approach will handle anything he could dream up."

"I'm sure it will, too," said Lisa. "You guys are very impressive. My only question is, which entry do you analyze first?"

Frank and Callie opened their mouths to answer at the same time, then looked at each other.

"Ladies first," said Frank.

"No, it's your computer," said Callie.

"Come *on*," Joe said impatiently.

"Okay," said Frank. "I figure we should check out the entry that appears the most times in the book. It probably represents one of the biggest bribers."

"As a matter of fact, I've already done it," said Callie. "This one comes up the most often." She pointed to an entry in the black book.

"One step ahead of me as usual," said Frank.

"As you said, ladies first," said Callie.

Frank typed the entry into his computer for the first analysis, then punched the command button.

He and the others leaned forward to watch the computer screen. In a second, various letter clusters appeared on the screen as the computer substituted the most frequently used letters of the alphabet for the most frequently used numbers in the code.

```
E___E          ___E___E
A___E          ___A___E
O___E          ___A___E
```

Joe grinned immediately. "We had to go through all this mumbo-jumbo to come up with something I had already figured out." He triumphantly jabbed his finger at the computer's second choice.

"Huh?" said Frank.

"Remember what I said earlier when we were studying the list of city contracts? I knew it was Acme Waste Disposal Corporation all the time."

"I hate to admit it," Frank said, "but I think you're right." He turned to Callie and Lisa. "Acme Waste Disposal Corporation was one of the firms that got big contracts from Bayport in the past year."

"Then there's no question that it's the one we should investigate first," said Lisa. "Hey, you're quite a guy, Joe." Her eyes gleamed with excitement.

"Well I just do my best to be great," said Joe.

"And so modest, too," said Callie.

"Now I hope you have the answer to another question," said Frank. "A big, nasty question."

"What's that?" asked Joe.

"If this bunch plays as rough as we think they do," asked Frank, "how do we go after Acme Waste without them wasting us?"

Chapter

12

IT WAS A busy morning for Mac Jessup, vice-president of Acme Waste Disposal Corporation. Mac Jessup was the person at Acme who gave the workers their instructions and the one to whom anyone looking for work was sent.

He was happy to see the first two job applicants that day. Business was growing, and they always needed new employees. Acme not only had the city contract, but it also had managed to get many private businesses to sign up for its services. Their sales pitch included the threat of possible fires and broken kneecaps if Acme didn't get the work.

The two job hunters who sat before him that morning looked like good prospects. They had strong backs and weak minds.

"I got no time for school," said the younger of the two, who said his name was Joe Johnson. He actually did feel bad about cutting school that day. But his case was too important. "Nothing they teach you there's gonna do you any good. Besides, all that reading makes my head hurt."

"Yeah," added his friend, Frank Davis. "I wanna get out and make bucks. Real bucks. And I don't care how dirty my hands get doing it."

"Well, kids, we pay well," said Mac, looking them over. "But we expect a few things in return."

"Don't worry 'bout that, man," said Joe. "Feel this." He flexed his arm to make a muscle that bulged against his grease-stained denim work shirt.

"We ain't afraid of hard work," Frank said. "We'll really put out if the money's right."

Mac smiled, revealing a set of crooked teeth that he meant to have straightened when he got his Christmas bonus that year. It would probably be a bundle. Acme Waste Disposal was really making money. And kids like these two could help it make even more.

"I'm not talking about muscle power," Mac told them. "I'm talking about brains. Enough brains to keep your mouth shut about your work. There's some stuff we don't like our competition or any other kind of snooper to know. It's what you call your corporate security."

Joe blinked, clearly trying to digest the words. "Oh, yeah, sure, corporate security. Yeah, sure."

Frank gave him a superior look. "Hey, dumbbell, he means, keep your lips buttoned if anybody asks you questions about anything."

Joe brightened. "You mean, like when the cops hauled us in and—" He shut his mouth when Frank punched him in the shoulder.

"Hey, Joe here don't mean it like it sounds," Frank apologized to Mac. "He was just giving you, like, a for-instance. We never had nothing to do with the cops, cross my heart."

Mac's smile grew even bigger. These two were perfect. "Don't worry about that, kids. We're real broad-minded about stuff like that here. You'll find that out soon enough."

"Hey, you mean we're hired?" asked Joe.

" 'Course that's what he means, jerko," Frank assured him.

"Ten dollars an hour—and twenty for night work," said Mac. "We get a lot of night work."

"Great," said Joe. "Since we cut out of school, I like sleeping late."

"When do we start?" asked Frank.

"Today," said Mac. "Come on, I'll show you the ropes."

But before he could lead them out of his office, another visitor barged in.

It took Mac a second to realize the intruder was

a woman, since she was dressed in men's clothes and wore a construction worker's hard hat.

Behind her, Mac's secretary made a helpless gesture.

"What do you want, lady?" Mac asked in a hostile voice.

"Don't call me lady," said the woman. "And what I want is a job."

"Sorry, we got all the secretaries and file clerks we need," said Mac. "This outfit ain't big on paperwork."

"I'm not, either," said the woman. "You can keep those low-paying jobs. I want one of the jobs that pays real money."

"Forget it," Mac answered. "That's men's work."

"Oh, yeah?" she said. "That's a real interesting remark. I'm sure the State Commission on Equal Rights would love to hear it." She pulled a small tape recorder out of her pocket. "You want to hire me? Or do you want some state officials to come nosing around here looking for an incident of discrimination against women?"

Mac's tone changed from sour to sweet. He tried his best to smile. "Look, miss, I don't want you to get the wrong idea. It's just that the work involves a lot of lifting and hauling. A pretty thing like you can't be expected to do that kind of labor."

"Oh, yeah?" The woman shifted a wad of gum

from one side of her mouth to the other. "Try me. I've been pumping iron for a year."

Mac cleared his throat. "Well, in that case—"

"My name's Lisa—Lisa Lee. Just so you know what name to put on my paycheck. And it better be for the same amount you're paying these guys." She turned to Joe and Frank. "How much you getting?"

Joe opened his mouth, but Frank punched him in the ribs before he could speak.

"We ain't at liberty to say," Frank said, looking to Mac for approval.

Mac nodded. "Good. You got the idea. Say nothing to nobody. And that goes for you, too, Lisa. You get hired, and you do the same work as all the men. You keep your mouth shut about everything that goes on here. Or maybe you got a problem with that?"

Lisa shrugged. "No problem, buster. You pay me the same, and I do the same. I need the bucks too bad."

"Ten bucks an hour—and twenty for night work," said Mac.

"You just bought yourself all the silence you want," said Lisa. "I warn you, though, if you want me to kill somebody, I'll expect a raise." Her expression indicated that she wasn't joking.

Mac's eyes softened. Maybe this dame would work out after all.

115

"Come on, let's put you three to work," said Mac, leading the way out of the office.

"You run this whole show?" Joe asked as they walked down the corridor of the small building that housed the Acme offices.

"Me run the show?" said Mac. "You'd be lucky if I did. I'm a real pussycat compared to the boss. You'll meet him tonight, before you go on your night shift. He gets final approval of all the people we hire, but he ain't showing up here until about seven. He's got a lot of interests all over, and he just checks in here a couple of times a week."

"We're working tonight, too?" said Lisa.

"Yeah," said Mac. "A split shift. Any objections? You still got time to quit. But after tonight, I gotta warn you, you ain't gonna be able to quit so easy. We got a real tough severance policy for trusted employees who try to cut out. It's not like we hand you a final paycheck. It's more like we hand you your head."

As Mac led them outside toward a high sheet-metal fence laced with electrified wiring, Joe and Frank glanced anxiously at Lisa to see how she had taken Mac's warning. She shrugged and said, "Night work is great with me. Just so long as you pay me like you said."

"We always pay like we say," said Mac, unlocking a gate in the middle of the fence.

Inside the enclosed area, metal barrels were being loaded onto trucks by grunting workmen. Mac led the three new employees of Acme Waste Disposal to a big bunch of barrels stacked four high. Then he pointed to a truck parked next to the barrels and told Frank, Joe, and Lisa to get to work.

"When you're finished, knock off," he said. "Give your time to the guy with the checkout sheet over there, then come back tonight at seven. I'll have the boss okay you, and then you can ride out on the truck and unload it."

"You unload it at night?" said Joe, shaking his head in puzzlement.

"When nobody can see the cargo, jerk," Frank said to him. Frank turned to Mac. "Am I right, or am I right?"

"You're a smart kid," said Mac. "Just don't get too smart for your own good. Remember, we're not paying you to think. We're paying you to sweat. And you can start right now."

Acme got its money's worth that afternoon. It took all three of them—Lisa, Joe, and Frank—working together to lift each barrel.

"I wonder what's in these," said Joe, grunting.

"I've got a hunch we wouldn't want to take a bath in whatever is sloshing around in there," said Frank.

Lisa was quiet as they worked.

"You've got real muscle," Joe commented. "Were you telling the truth about pumping iron?"

"I do work out a little bit," Lisa replied. "It's to burn up calories—I have a sinful weakness for chocolate-chip cookies."

At three they were finished. Lisa wiped the sweat off her forehead and said with a grin, "I can eat a whole box of cookies now and not feel guilty."

"We actually have some at our place," said Frank. "Let's get something to eat there, before coming back here. Callie must be waiting for us."

"I hope she isn't still mad about not being able to come," said Lisa.

"She has to know it was no-go," said Joe. "She looks too fragile. No way she could have convinced them to take her on. I have to admit, I even had doubts about you. Looks like I was wrong. You keep amazing me more and more. I've never met a girl like you."

"I'll take that as a compliment," said Lisa, smiling. "I just hope I can get by the interview with the big boss tonight. After that, we can really find out what Acme is into and see if we can pick up any leads on the killing. The more they trust us, the more they're likely to let information spill."

Back at the Hardys' the four sat around the kitchen table destroying all the leftovers in the refrigerator plus all the cookies in the cupboard. Frank was filling Callie in on what had happened.

"So you see," he said, "it's really important you stay behind. If we're caught, we'll need you. We have to be able to tell them that we have somebody who'll go to the cops if something happens to us."

"You guys just want to have all the fun," Callie said angrily.

"I know how you feel, Callie," said Joe. "Being stuck here would drive me nuts. But we need you. Okay?"

Callie shrugged. "Do I have a choice?"

In the van on the way back to Acme, Frank turned to Lisa. "I think this is where the action's really going to start," he said. "Are you ready?"

"I think so," said Lisa. "I just hope I can keep up with you guys."

"From what you've shown me so far," Joe told her, "there's no worry about that." He smiled at her in the rearview mirror.

"Thanks," said Lisa. "You sure know how to make a girl feel good." She smiled back. Their gazes locked.

"Hey, you two," Frank cut in, "let's pay attention to the job at hand. We still have to see the boss before we can probe any deeper into Acme."

But when they arrived at Acme they didn't get

to see the boss. Mac led them into an empty room.

"This is where the boss does his interviewing," he said.

"And when does he get here?" asked Lisa. "Not that I care—as long as I'm being paid for the time I have to wait."

"You don't got to wait at all," said Mac. "The boss is already here. And he's already checking you out."

Mac smirked at their puzzled expressions, then pointed to a peephole in the wall.

"The boss likes his privacy," he explained. "The fewer people who see his face, the better it is for everybody. Especially them. It ain't so healthy to know too much about the boss."

"So we get interviewed from the other side of a wall?" said Lisa.

"You just *been* interviewed," said Mac. "The boss ain't crazy about people hearing his voice, either. Like I said, he's a real private kind of guy. He just likes to give new people a quick once-over, in case they send off bad vibes or ring a bell he doesn't want to hear."

He grinned. "The boss is very, very sharp about stuff like that. That's how he's done so good. He's never let the wrong kind of person get close to him. Nobody's ever been able to finger him for anything."

"When do we know if we passed?" asked Frank.

"In a minute," answered Mac. "I'll check with him." He paused at the door. "Oh, yeah, I forgot. Don't even think about trying to leave. There's a guy outside the door who wouldn't be happy if you did."

"And if we flunk out?" asked Lisa.

"He's gonna be even more unhappy," said Mac. "We don't like to let the people who might bad-mouth our company go. The boss says it's bad PR."

"So we just stand here and wait for you to make up your mind," said Joe. "I don't go for that."

"You want to do something, I'll tell you what to do," said Mac. He glowered at this punk kid as his voice shifted to a snarl. "You can pray."

121

Chapter

13

JOE GLANCED AT Lisa, standing beside him and Frank. He wished she was still carrying the guns she had picked up. They could use them then—if the mysterious boss was as sharp as Mac had said. But they had decided to leave the guns behind. It would have been out of character for Lisa Lee to carry a shoulder bag, and her work clothes left no room for a concealed weapon. Maybe they'd been too cautious for their own good. Now they were sitting ducks if anything went wrong.

The door opened. Joe and the others tensed.

"Okay, kids," Mac said. "We got a lot of work hustling those barrels tonight. Let's get moving."

"First you keep us waiting, then you tell us to hurry up," said Joe, careful not to show the relief that came flooding through him. "It's just like my dad said the army was."

"As far as you're concerned, you are in an army—and you follow orders," said Mac as they left the building and headed for the enclosure.

Waiting at the truck were two men, one dark and one blond, both with beards and both built like pro football fullbacks.

"This is Mike," said Mac, indicating the black-haired one. "And Fred," indicating the other. "They're working with you on the unloading. This part of the job has to be done as fast as we can dump the stuff. I'm going along, too, just to see how you do. You three ride in back. Us three will go in front."

"We got a long drive to the dumping ground?" asked Frank.

"Shut your mouth, open your eyes, and you'll see," Mac answered as he climbed behind the wheel. The other two men squeezed in beside him in the driver's cabin.

Joe, Frank, and Lisa climbed onto the back of the flatbed truck. They were barely able to jam themselves into the small area that was left empty behind the barrels. Mac started up the truck.

"Good thing these barrels are tightly secured under the tarp," whispered Frank. "I'd hate to have one of these babies topple over on me."

"Let's hope the road isn't too rough, and the trip isn't too long," said Lisa.

"Yeah," said Joe. "Mac is driving like a cowboy—he hasn't even put on his headlights. Do you suppose he doesn't want anyone to see this truck?"

"Can't imagine why," Frank answered dryly.

The bone-jarring ride lasted less than a half-hour. The truck came to a stop, and almost instantly Mac, Mike, and Fred were out of the cab and standing behind the truck looking up at Joe, Frank, and Lisa.

"Get the tarp off and get to work," Mac commanded. "You hand the barrels down to us, and we'll stack them."

Joe, Frank, and Lisa untied the ropes holding the tarp down, and removed it from the barrels. Then they started wrestling the barrels, one by one, to the edge of the flatbed. There they tipped each barrel over on its side and rolled it gently over the edge into the waiting hands of Mike and Fred, who then rolled it off into the darkness. After more than an hour of grunting effort, they were almost done. Only three barrels were left. They all gathered around the nearest one and tensed their muscles as they prepared to grab it.

"Okay," said Frank. "All together now, one, two, three—"

Suddenly he and the others were thrown off balance, nearly tripping over their own feet as their effort sent the barrel spinning on the flatbed surface.

"It's light as a feather," said Joe.

"It's empty," said Frank, rapping his knuckles on it and hearing a hollow sound. He checked the others. They were empty, too.

"What's the deal with these?" Lisa asked Mac, who was watching what was going on, his flashlight illuminating the action.

Mac shrugged. "Some kind of goof-up."

"You want them off, too?" Joe asked.

"Yeah, why not," said Mac. "We don't get a deposit back for returning empties."

They passed the barrels down to Mike and Fred and Mac, who volunteered to roll the last one away.

Before Mac did, he said, "Get off the truck and follow us."

Joe, Frank, and Lisa jumped off the flatbed. As they followed Mac they saw his flashlight cutting through the darkness and for the first time realized where they were.

"Some kind of water," said Lisa.

"It's Barmet Bay," said Joe. "I know this cove. It's a great place to swim in the summertime. Super fishing, too."

"Yeah, some of the fish are real big," said Frank. "The bay is a good breeding ground. Parts of it are real deep."

"That's why we're here," said Mac as they reached a ramshackle wooden wharf. Mac rolled his barrel to where the other barrels were stacked. Mike and Fred were already loading one of them into a large rowboat moored there.

"You mean you dump this stuff in the bay?" asked Joe—even though he already knew the answer.

"Smart kid," said Mac. "It's a perfect setup. This place is a short drive from town, which cuts down on the transportation costs. It's deep enough to hold all we can dump into it. And there's nobody to charge us for using it. Like they say, the best things in life are free."

"But if those drums leak, they'll trace it back to you, I mean, us," said Frank, thinking how he had been swimming in Barmet Bay the past summer, and how he was planning to swim there again next summer. He thought of the stuff in the barrels—and started changing his plans.

"Leak? What you mean?" Mac said with mock indignation. "These are good barrels. Guaranteed not to leak—not for four or five years. By that time Acme Waste Disposal will be long gone."

"But the fish and the swimmers won't be," muttered Joe.

"Not immediately, anyway." Mac chuckled. Then he looked suspiciously at Joe, who was staring at the lake and shaking his head. "Hey, what's the matter, kid? Got cold feet? Don't want to get your pretty white hands dirty with nasty work?"

"Ain't that," Joe said casually. "The thing is, though, with what I know now, I gotta figure my work should be worth more. I'm running an extra risk, getting mixed up with the law."

"Don't worry about the law," said Mac. "We got our ways of handling that."

"You mean the city manager?" asked Frank. "Yeah, I heard about him being on the take. But he's dead now."

Mac shrugged. "So we'll find somebody else."

"Know what?" Lisa said. "I heard that the guy didn't do himself in. I heard somebody rubbed him out. You guys mixed up in that? 'Cause if you're into heavy stuff like that, I'm with Joe. I want more money."

Mac grinned at her. But it wasn't a pleasant grin. It was more like the grin of a shark. "You're real curious. Not to mention greedy. But I'll show you the kind of guy I am. I was going to wait until later, when you finished helping us dump this stuff, before I settled up with you. But since you're so eager, I'll give you what's coming to you now, just so you don't walk out on me."

Suddenly Joe, Frank, and Lisa were staring at a gun in Mac's hand. A long-barreled gun, with a bulging silencer fitted over the barrel.

"Hey, man, just because we shot off our mouths a little, there's no reason to get upset," Joe said.

"Yeah," said Lisa. "I was just feeling you out

for a little more money, but I wasn't serious. You can't blame a girl for trying."

"We're sorry," Frank added. "You know how it is with kids like us. Sometimes we step out of line."

"Sure, I know how it is with kids like you," said Mac, keeping his gun leveled at them. Without turning his head away from them, he shouted, "Mike! Fred! Come on over here! It's payoff time!"

In an instant Fred and Mike were at his side. Their faces were blank, even bored, as if this were just another routine job, as easy and unexciting as rolling barrels.

Mac, however, was positively gloating. "You kids thought you were smart, huh, smarter than the boss. You thought he was some kind of patsy."

"Us?" said Joe.

"Not on your life," said Frank.

"We don't even know who the boss is," said Lisa.

"You bet you don't," said Mac, enjoying it more and more. "Let me tell you what kind of guy the boss is. If he hears that a company he partially owns—like Eat-Right—has a missing manager, he checks it out right away. He hears from a receptionist that a couple of snoopy high school kids visited it yesterday afternoon, right out of the blue. So he has that receptionist with him when some high school kids come to his offices tonight. And when that receptionist identifies one of them right away, he figures out what to do right away, too."

Mac paused to let his words sink in. Then he went on, "And here's the beautiful part. Not only does he get a free night's work out of the kids, and not only does he find a perfect place to get rid of them—he even has them unload their own coffins."

Mac smacked his gun against the barrel he had rolled down the wharf. It gave off a hollow gong.

"Of course, the barrels will be a tight fit," said Mac. "But we'll be able to stuff you in them while you're still limp, before you start to stiffen up."

While Mac was talking, Joe let his eyes flick in Frank's direction, careful not to change the scared expression on his face. His gaze met Frank's.

It wasn't the first time the Hardys had faced guns. But this time they had only one weapon with which to defend themselves.

Surprise.

The Hardys knew that no one holding a gun would anticipate an unarmed person charging him.

Joe went for him right then, and out of the corner of his eye saw Frank doing the same.

In fact, on his other side, he sensed that was Lisa going for him, too.

129

The gun spat fire, but there wasn't a deafening bang—just a sound like hands clapping. Joe tensed, but he knew the shot had missed him. He prayed it had missed Lisa and Frank, too. Joe hit Mac knee-high, and in the same movement reached up to grab the gun in Mac's hand. Before Joe could twist it up and away, another shot went off.

Mac went down moaning as Joe's fist connected with his chin. The gun flew into the air. A few feet from it, Frank was delivering a beautiful karate chop to Fred's neck. Fred was already holding his forearm as if it had been smashed, and now he toppled forward, out like a light.

Mike, too, was doubled up in pain, lying on the ground and groaning from a kick from Lisa's shoe. "Good work, Lisa," Joe said. "That guy is out."

Joe was about to bend over to pick up Mac's gun when he heard Mac's voice. "You've had it, punk!"

Joe whirled around. Mac was lying on his stomach with another gun in his hand.

A gun that was pointed straight at Joe.

A gun that was going to go off before Joe or Frank or Lisa had a chance of stopping him.

"Die!" Mac bellowed with rage.

Chapter
14

JOE TENSED FOR the sound of a shot and the impact of a bullet slamming into him.

But all he heard was Mac's bellow of rage turn into a scream.

A scream of pain.

Mac's face was a mask of agony. His gun hand was clenched in a fist. The gun itself had dropped to the wharf.

Before he could recover, Joe, Frank, and Lisa had reached him. Frank and Joe each grabbed him by an arm, while Lisa scooped up the gun.

Mac whimpered and said in a small, babyish voice, "It *hurts!*"

Joe looked down at Mac's hand and saw what Mac meant. The skin on the back of the hand was an unsightly mess of red and blistered flesh.

Frank whistled. "Look at that."

In the barrel behind Mac a stream of liquid was gushing out from a bullet hole. Joe glanced down at the wooden planking where the liquid was falling. Already the wood had been eaten away. Somehow, when he raised his gun to fire, that liquid had spattered onto Mac's hand.

"You're lucky," Joe said to Mac. "Think what it'd be like to swim in that stuff."

"Yeah, now all you're in is hot water," said Lisa. While Joe and Frank held Mac tightly by the arms, Lisa pressed the gun firmly against his forehead, right between the eyes. "I suggest you cooperate with us—if you don't want to get in any deeper."

"Hey, whatever you say," said Mac, his pain forgotten in his sudden panic. "Be careful of that thing, okay? The trigger is sensitive. The least little thing will set it off."

"And the least little thing will set *me* off," said Lisa. "So tell me what I want to know, and don't even think of lying."

"You've got my word," Mac said, looking wide-eyed and panicky.

"Did you or your boss engineer Morrison's murder?" she asked. "Talk, and talk fast."

"Honest, I don't know nothing about it!" said Mac, his face twitching. "I'm just smallfry at Acme. The boss don't let me in on stuff like that."

"And where can we find your boss right now?" Lisa persisted.

"Back in the office," said Mac. "He said he was gonna wait for me to make sure the job tonight went off without a hitch."

"Your boss does all his dirty work that way?" said Lisa. "Hires other people to do it for him?"

"Yeah, that's his style," said Mac.

"If you're not telling the truth—" Lisa said threateningly as she tapped the end of the gun against Mac's forehead.

"Honest! I swear!" Mac managed to choke out.

"I guess we've gotten all we can out of him," Lisa said to Joe and Frank.

"Hey, you really know how to give the third-degree," whispered Joe. "You were making *me* nervous—and I'm on your side!"

"Part of a reporter's training," Lisa said coolly. "But now the one we have to interview is Mac's boss. I've got a hunch he's the one with the answers."

"First we have to figure out what to do with Mac. Not to mention Fred and Mike here," said Frank, indicating the two thugs who were still lying unconscious.

"We can haul them to the truck and tie them up with the ropes that were holding down the tarp," said Lisa. "We can do the same thing with Mac."

"Good idea," said Joe. He stooped and

grabbed Fred underneath his arms and started to drag him toward the truck. Frank did the same with Mike. Lisa took up the rear, herding Mac in front of her at gunpoint.

With the three crooks tied up and gagged under the tarp in the back of the flatbed, they drove back to the Acme offices. They parked a couple of blocks away.

"We can leave these guys here," said Lisa. "I don't think they're going anywhere, not the way you tied them up. You sure know your knots. What were you, Boy Scouts?"

"We were—until we got too busy with other activities," said Frank.

"Yeah," said Joe. "Too bad the Boy Scouts didn't give merit badges for busting bad guys. Frank and I would have been super Eagle Scouts."

"I bet you would have," said Lisa. "Well, here's your chance to add a nifty prize to your collection. The Acme boss sounds like he's real big-time."

"I just hope he's the one who did the killing," said Frank. "Otherwise my dad's file room is going to get pretty crowded."

"Yeah. We'll have to buy another case of cat food," said Joe.

There wasn't a sign of life inside as they approached the Acme building.

"Now we'll find out if Mac was telling the truth and his boss is still waiting here," said Frank as he began to work on picking the lock on the door. Lisa pulled out the gun that she had taken from Mac and held it at the ready.

"We're in," whispered Frank as the lock tumblers clicked. He turned the handle, and the door swung open. They moved inside the dark building.

"Here's the room where we were interviewed," Frank said softly. "If the boss was looking at us through a peephole, this next room could be the one he's in."

"There's only one way to find out," Joe whispered back.

"Right," Lisa replied with a sudden decisiveness that startled both Frank and Joe.

She grabbed the doorknob, swung open the door, and stepped inside with her gun pointed into the room.

"Freeze," she commanded in a voice as hard as nails.

"D-d-don't shoot," called a voice from within.

Lisa stepped into the brightly lit room and Frank and Joe followed.

"Shut the door quickly," she said, without turning her head. "We don't want to be interrupted."

Frank did so, careful not to make any noise,

135

then turned around to look at the man sitting behind a big mahogany desk.

"Stand up, so we can get a good look at you," Lisa said, her voice edged with menace.

His face pale with fear, the man followed the order instantly. When he snapped to his feet, it was as if he were riding an elevator upward. He was tall, very tall—almost seven feet—and impeccably dressed in a gray suit. His shirt was silk, with wide pale blue stripes, and his tie was a conservative navy blue. Gold cuff links gleamed at the edge of his sleeves.

This well-dressed man would have looked right at home in the office of a corporate executive or, for that matter, in an English country manor house.

But his voice didn't match his polished appearance. Although he spoke with a distinguished accent, his speech was marred by a persistent stutter.

"W-w-what are you doing here?" he asked. "Are you thieves? If so, you are out of l-l-luck. There's no c-c-cash in this office, and I carry only c-c-credit cards."

"What we want is information," said Lisa. "About the killing of Jack Morrison. You did it, right? Or I should say, ordered it—since we've heard you don't like to get your hands dirty."

"You're r-r-right," said the Acme boss. Then

he smiled. "F-f-fortunately, I have very g-g-good hired h-h-hands."

"Aghhh," Lisa cried as an arm from behind suddenly snaked around her neck and wrestled the gun from her hand.

Before Joe and Frank could move to help her, she was flung to the center of the room, and the Hardys found themselves facing a huge man in a black suit. He had Lisa's gun in one hand and his own gun in the other.

"G-g-good work, Sam." The boss sat down again behind the desk. Then he sneered. "Did you k-k-kids really think it was th-th-that easy to break in here? D-d-didn't you ever hear about s-s-silent alarms? I j-j-just let you get this far to find out wh-wh-what was on your t-t-tiny minds. Now that I know, it is t-t-terribly simple to d-d-decide what to do with you."

Sam expressed himself more directly. "Line up against the wall," he commanded. After the Hardys and Lisa had followed his order, he turned to his boss, "You want me to knock them off here or someplace else?"

"It w-w-would be m-m-messy here—stain the carpet and all," the boss replied, putting a cigarette in a holder and lighting it with a slender gold lighter. "On the other h-h-hand, I'm planning to red-d-decorate, and I do want to see for myself that these intruders are d-d-disposed of once and for all. So you have my p-p-permission to do the nasty d-d-deed here, Sam."

"My pleasure." Sam grinned.

Joe and Frank exchanged hopeless glances. Sam was too far away to charge. And too close to miss them with whichever gun he chose to use.

It was all over—unless Lisa had a way to get them out of the mess.

She did her best.

"Look, can't we make a deal?" she asked.

"What kind of d-d-deal?" said the boss. His voice indicated that he knew perfectly well she was playing for time, and he was enjoying the attempt the same way he might enjoy watching a fish wiggling on a hook.

"I've got something you want—something you want very much," said Lisa.

"And wh-wh-what's that, my d-d-dear?" asked the boss in an even more sardonic tone.

"I'll show you," said Lisa, her voice quivering with terror as she reached into the deep pocket of her workpants.

Joe and Frank's mouths dropped open. Lisa whipped out a gun, and in the same motion let off a shot.

The shot was a barely audible thumping sound.

The only loud noise was the sound of Sam screaming as the bullet tore past his ear.

Joe got the picture in a flash. Lisa had pocketed the first gun Mac had pulled on them, the one Joe had knocked out of his hand—the gun with the silencer on it. She must have done it when he and Frank were hauling the two knocked-out crooks back to the truck.

This time she didn't bother picking up the two guns that Sam had dropped. She merely kicked them to one side as she motioned with her gun for Sam to stand beside the desk.

Then she pointed her gun at the boss. "Don't even think about reaching into your drawer," she said. "I missed Sam because I wanted to. But I can just as easily get *you*—right between the eyes."

"You'd better believe it." Joe backed her up.

Lisa ignored him. Her attention was still focused on the boss and Sam. "You two stand right there against the wall," she said to them.

"Yeah, you can take our places." Joe grinned.

"Right, be our guests," said Frank, sighing with relief. This was one tight spot he hadn't been able to see a way out of.

Both Hardys couldn't believe their eyes when they saw Lisa's gun swivel toward them.

Just as they couldn't believe their ears when she said in an icy voice, "Who said you two could move? *Freeze*."

Joe gasped.

She had to be joking.

But she wasn't.

The gun she had trained on them told him that.

Chapter

15

JOE STOOD WITH his hands held high over his head and his back against the wall. On his left was Frank, in the same posture. And on his right stood the Acme boss and his goon, Sam.

Joe looked at Lisa as she faced them with a gun in her hand, but he could barely recognize her. She no longer looked like a young woman in her early twenties, much less like the teenager she had disguised herself as the day before. There was nothing sunny and fresh about her face now. Her expression was ice cold, and her face was etched with sharp lines and edges. Joe could see that she was about thirty, if not older. She might have a lot of faces, but he was sure that this one was her real one, whoever she might actually be.

The Acme boss knew who she was.

"It's y-y-*you*," he gasped. "Gina."

"Fast thinking," Lisa said in a voice as hard as her face.

"Gina?" asked Joe.

"It's what you might call my professional name," she said.

"A v-v-very well-known name in her profession," said the Acme boss.

"By the way, not that it matters, but what's *your* name?" asked Gina. "I've been curious about you since you hired me—and even more curious lately."

"E-E-Elliot. Elliot S-S-Saunders, the Third," the tall man said. "But how did you find me?"

"You can thank these two kids here," Gina said. "They're really good at hunting down people. I would have had a tough time doing it without them. Of course, you helped me, too— just by opening your mouth. All I had to do was hear that stutter of yours to know that you were the guy who'd hired me over the phone."

She sneered. "You thought you were being so smart not to give me your name. You should have been smart enough to have somebody else do your talking." She permitted herself a thin, tight smile. "Elliot Saunders, the Third, huh? Got any kids?"

"No," said Saunders. Sweat was streaming down his aristocratic forehead.

"Too bad," said Gina. "Then you're going to be Elliot Saunders, the Last."

Elliot started to lower one hand to wipe his brow but a jerk of Gina's gun was all it took for him to raise his hand high again. He had to stand there, blinking away the sweat as it dripped into his eyes. It looked like he was trying not to cry.

"B-b-but why on earth do you want to k-k-kill me?" Saunders pleaded. "We're both on the same side."

"The only side I'm on is my own," said Gina, her voice growing harder. "I'm not a pro for nothing. I haven't survived in this business by trusting people. As soon as I heard that the cops were on to the killing, I knew I had to cover my tracks. And I had to do it fast—before they got any further in their investigation of Morrison's funny business. You have to die because you're the one who hired me. You're the only one who knows my name."

"Y-y-you don't actually think I'd squeal on you," said Saunders, trying to sound indignant. He sounded more like a squeaking mouse.

"You'd do anything to have them shave a few years off your sentence," said Gina contemptuously. "You would have sold me down the river without thinking twice about it."

"I-I-I tell you you're wrong," said Saunders. "Look, if it's more money you want—"

"If I'm wrong, it's too bad—for you," said Gina with a shrug. "As for money, I'll be satisfied with the down payment you deposited in my account. I'll take the loss on the rest. I'll just have to pull a few more hits next year to make up for it."

She gave him another nasty smile. "It really hurts me right now, though, doing all these free-bies. Let's see, there'll be you and your goon, these two kids, the three guys tied up in the truck, then their friend Callie, and last but not least, the couple of guys locked up at their house. It's like a going-out-of-business sale. Except, of course, for me it means staying in business and out of the pen. So I guess it has to be worth it."

Joe shook his head, stunned. He felt like some-body was using his brain as a punching bag. There was a hollow feeling in his gut, too. Nice going, Joe, he said to himself. You really picked a winner this time.

Next to him, Frank wore an intense expression as his mind worked on this puzzle as if it were the last thing he would ever do. He nodded as it all came together for him.

"I get it now," he said.

Gina looked at him. "Well, well, Sherlock here has figured it all out," she said, sneering. "Why don't you clue your brother in. I owe you both that much for helping me out."

"Saunders hired you to kill Morrison, make it look like a suicide, and steal the black book containing his list of payoffs before it could be used as evidence in the investigation of corruption," said Joe. "Right?"

"Almost," said Gina. "Except that Saunders didn't know about the black book. I found it in Morrison's desk after I knocked him off. I saw how much it would be worth and pocketed it. Figured I could sell it for a bundle. Then Callie crashed into me at City Hall, and she got her hands on it."

Gina's lips thinned again. "I figured out what had happened too late, so I had to hang around the high school until I spotted her. Then I trailed her until I got the chance to grab it back. I followed her to her house and then to yours, but it wasn't until she left to go back home alone that I could make my move."

"But she didn't have it on her," said Frank, almost forgetting the spot he was in as he eagerly put together the pieces. "So you ransacked her house and weren't able to find it there. You didn't find it until you spotted us with it from outside Callie's window. That's when you turned out the lights and grabbed it."

"Hey, you get a gold star," said Gina. "You're going to be the biggest brain in the cemetery."

"But one thing I don't understand," said Frank, still immersed in unraveling the puzzle. "Once you had the black book, why did you go through the bit about being a reporter attacked by a mugger?"

"I'm sure if you thought a bit, you'd figure it out," said Gina. "But seeing that you're not going to have the time for that, I'll fill you in. I wanted to know how much you kids had found out from the black book. If it turned out to be anything at all, I was going to ask for a bonus for making three extra hits."

"Right. It all makes sense now," Frank muttered.

Joe looked at Frank. "Yeah. Too bad it didn't come clear a little sooner." His face set like a stone as he looked at Gina. "You really had me fooled. Clever—those do-it-yourself bruises on your neck convinced me that someone tried to strangle you. But why didn't you leave us alone after that, when we found out Callie's notes had been destroyed? Why team up with us to find out who was involved in the payoffs?"

Gina looked at Frank. "Should I tell him or do you want to? You don't have to answer that—I can see you're dying to. Just make it fast. Time's a-wasting, and I've got a lot of work to do tonight."

Her reminder made Frank gulp. But he still went on, caught up in the rush of his logic. "It's simple. As soon as Gina learned that the fake suicide she'd staged to mask Morrison's murder hadn't worked, she knew the cops would start hunting for a killer. So she had to cover her tracks. That meant wiping out the one person who could name her: the person who hired her. But she didn't know who he was. She only knew him by his voice. She had to find him, and to do that she had to find out who had been making the payoffs, and we offered the help she needed."

"I've got it now," said Joe, caught up in Frank's flow of ideas despite his pending fate. "And when Karnovsky at Eat-Right turned out not to be the one she was looking for, she made sure that we got the black book back so we could decode it for her and help her check out the other suspects."

"Hey, Joe, you're not as dumb as I thought you were," said Gina. "Of course, nobody could be *that* dumb and still breathe. Which, I'm real sad to say, you and your bright brother are about to stop doing."

"Hey," said Joe desperately. "Don't we get any last requests?"

"Sure," said Gina. "You can tell me who wants to get it first. You or your brother. After I get rid of Saunders and Sam here, of course."

"A-a-any k-k-kind of m-m-money you w-w-want," pleaded Saunders pitifully.

Gina responded with a cold stare.

"I'm just a working guy, like you," Sam said, his voice hoarse with fear.

Gina shrugged.

"Hey, you'd better look out behind you!" Frank said suddenly.

At this, Gina began to smile. "I'd have expected a better trick from you, smart boy." Her pistol flicked over to Frank. "Did you really think I would turn around? Dumb, dumb, dumb. That just earned you the number-one spot in my hit parade."

Chapter

16

GINA WAS STILL laughing as her finger tightened on the trigger. "The oldest, corniest trick in the b—

"Ugh," she grunted as Callie brought the baseball bat down across the back of her head. Gina tumbled to the floor.

Joe let Saunders get a head start in the race for the gun that dropped from Gina's hand. Then he stuck out his foot to send Saunders sprawling to the floor. Joe was on top of him in a flash. His arm snaked around Saunders's windpipe, and he tightened his hold until Saunders gasped, "Enough. You w-w-win."

Meanwhile Frank grabbed one of Sam's arms as the big thug dashed for the gun. Using Sam's forward momentum, Frank flipped him forward, to send him crashing headfirst into a wall. Sam staggered groggily to his feet, then, as his eyes rolled backward, he collapsed in a heap.

Joe yanked Saunders to his feet and pushed him toward the wall, next to Sam. "What we need now," Joe said, "is something to tie them all up with."

"We can use the telephone wire, for a start," Frank said, quickly unclipping it. Saunders protested, but he was soon bound hand and foot.

"And I know just the thing for Gina and Sam," Callie said. "It'll be my pleasure to go get it." Handing the baseball bat to Joe, she dashed out of the room but soon returned with a spool of electrical wire.

Once Sam and Gina were safely trussed and a phone call made to police headquarters, the Hardys and Callie were finally able to talk about what had happened.

"I couldn't believe it when I saw you sneaking through the door with that bat in your hand," Frank told her.

"And *I* couldn't believe it when I heard you tell Gina to look out behind her," said Callie, shaking her head.

"I did that to keep her from looking around, in case you made a noise or one of us gave you away," Frank explained. "I knew Gina would never believe a corny line like that."

Callie gave him a long stare. "I know you're

smart, Frank—but sometimes you're too smart for comfort." She broke into a grin. "I almost died when I heard you shout."

"I'll never tell you that you're too smart for our comfort," Frank grinned back. "If you hadn't been, we would have been killed."

"Hey, Callie," Joe said. "Great wrist action with my bat! I never thought I'd be this happy to see you!"

Callie answered sharply. "No, I'm sure you didn't. Please—save your applause," she cut both Hardys off as they tried to speak. "You had your perfect team here—with old Callie sitting home by the phone. Of course, one of the team turned out to be the bad guy. I'm kind of glad I didn't join up."

Joe's face darkened. He opened his mouth to make an angry reply, then shut it, turning to his brother. "What can I say?" he asked, shrugging. "She's right."

"She sure is," Frank agreed. "Callie, how did you know we were going to be in trouble? I mean, what made you trail us here tonight?"

"Well, I had a feeling that Lisa—I mean Gina—was a little too good to be true," Callie answered him. "It was just too much of a coincidence, the same person attacking both of us."

Callie frowned. "See, there was no real reason for him to go after her. When she said the guy only tried to snatch her purse, the first time you met her, I began to wonder. All the attacks on me were so much more elaborate. It didn't add up. And another thing: On the night when we were 'mugged' together on the way home, I could have sworn there was no one near us."

"The idea of mugging *is* to take the victim by surprise," Joe said dryly.

"Yes, but I wasn't exactly daydreaming. I was on the lookout for something like that, and I had trouble believing anyone could sneak up on both of us that completely."

"Great thinking!" Frank said. He put his arms around Callie. "You really saved our lives," he said, looking into her eyes. "I don't know how to thank you."

"Don't worry. I'll help you think of something," Callie said, her eyes twinkling.

Joe cleared his throat. "Uh, Callie, I want to thank you, too. And I'd like to, um, apologize for underestimating you. For a girl"—he stopped as Callie glared at him—"I mean, for a beginner— for *anyone*—you did a great job. We'd be in a lot of trouble without you."

"Apology accepted. With pleasure," said Callie. A smile lurked at the corners of her mouth. "By the way," she added casually, "there's one more reason I thought Gina had to be a fake."

"What's that?" asked Joe.

"You really want to know?" Callie asked.

"Yeah, I really want to know," said Joe.

"Okay, you asked," said Callie. "All I had to do was see a woman like Gina making gaga eyes at a guy like you, and I could be absolutely sure *something* wasn't for real."

"Good deduction," said Frank, nodding seriously.

"Hey, wait a minute!" Joe began.

Then Frank and Callie burst out laughing. After a moment Joe joined them. "I know you've been saving that one for a long time," he said to Callie. "Okay, welcome to the team. But I'm putting you on special assignment."

"As what?" Callie asked suspiciously.

"I saw how you used this thing." Joe tapped the baseball bat. "I think you should be our designated hitter!"

Frank and Joe's next case:

The Hardys are after a gang of bank robbers—who do their stealing by computer! Evidence suggests that the thieves may be operating from the posh Chartwell Academy, so Frank goes undercover as a preppy.

He finds lots of suspects and lots of trouble—from an angry jock, to a gorgeous girl with a jealous boyfriend, to a computer nerd who has all the smarts to pull off the crime Frank is investigating. What's more, Joe is on the outside, having flunked the tough admissions exam.

Still worse, Frank's cover is no secret from the crooks. They want him off campus—or else. Will Frank and Joe make the grade on this case? Or will they flunk fatally? Find out in *The Genius Thieves*, Case #9 in The Hardy Boys Casefiles.